ALIENS & OTHER STORIES

Aliens
& Other Stories

Kathleen Wheaton

To Janis
with best wishes
Kathleen Wheaton

Washington Writers Publishing House
Washington, DC

THIS IS A WORK OF FICTION

Copyright © 2013 by Kathleen Wheaton

COVER DESIGN by Katrina Walter

BOOK DESIGN and TYPESETTING by Barbara Shaw

COVER PHOTOGRAPH by Pablo Corral Vega/
                    National Geographic Stock

AUTHOR PHOTOGRAPH by David Welna

LIBRARY OF CONGRESS CATALOGUING-IN-PUBLICATION DATA
Wheaton, Kathleen.
  [Short stories. Selections]
  Aliens and Other Stories / by Kathleen Wheaton.
     pages cm
  Includes bibliographical references.
  Short stories.
  ISBN 978-0-931846-71-7 (paperback : alk. paper)
  I. Title.
  PS3623.H425A78 2013
  813'.6—dc23

                                        2013019317

"Retrato"
by Antonio Machado
© 1940 Estate of Antonio Machado

Printed in the United States of America

WASHINGTON WRITERS' PUBLISHING HOUSE
P. O. Box 15271
Washington, D.C. 20003

FOR DAVID

CONTENTS

AUTHOR'S NOTE: Several of the stories in this volume refer to the "dirty war" in Argentina, which began in 1976 when a right-wing military junta overthrew the chaotic presidency of Isabel Peron. Under the so-called National Reorganization Process, an estimated 30,000 people—suspected leftist guerillas, trade unionists, journalists, intellectuals and students—were arrested, taken to clandestine prisons, tortured, and secretly executed. They became known as the *desaparecidos*, the disappeared. Although democracy was restored in 1983 with the election of President Raul Alfonsín, many of the thousands of Argentineans who fled into exile established their lives elsewhere and never returned.

"During that whole, long time, when we were away, I used to dream that I was coming home. Almost every night, for a long time, I dreamed that I was coming home. I still dream that I am coming home."

–Deborah Eisenberg, *Twilight of the Superheroes*

You Don't Know Anything

"Poor things," my mother murmured, hurrying me past the docks in Buenos Aires, where brown, wiry boys hoisted gunny sacks and shouted to each other in Sicilian.

"Why don't they go to school?"

"Well, my love, they're immigrants."

As if we weren't. But we didn't think of ourselves that way. My father had managed to persuade my mother, pregnant with me, to get on a boat for Argentina in the nick of time. She and I waited for him, and finally stopped waiting, in an apartment on Calle Bolivar, opposite a pastry shop. I was a fat boy, who wept over minor disappointments, and these two facts represented my mother's personal victory over the Nazis.

In Buenos Aires, you didn't hear German on the street. Jews avoided it because it had been Hitler's language; the others from our country, lying low, for the same reason. I believed, when I was small, that my mother had made it up. By the time I was in school, it was simply the language of reprimand.

I brought a girl to the apartment on Bolivar when I was sixteen. My mother was out, giving a piano lesson, a detail I didn't reveal to Leticia until we were standing in our kitchen, which, I noticed for the first time, smelled of boiled milk and laundry.

"So? I'm not exactly afraid of you." Leticia flipped her dark hair over her shoulder. She was one of the first to wear it long and straight.

I showed her the black-and-white photographs which were the pretext for her visit. They were pictures I'd taken along Avenida de Mayo, shot from angles that made my subjects loom ominously: a pigeon, a discarded newspaper, striding trouser legs.

"Good, good," Leticia said, nodding as she thumbed through them, like a policeman checking documents. She was known at school as *artística*, a broad-spectrum word that contained the rumor that she'd slept with a university student.

I'd considered various ways the conversation might go once she'd approved the pictures. "Do you think you'd go to bed with me?" I heard myself say.

Leticia burst out laughing. "Do you mean now, or in theory?"

The only possible thing was to act as though my question

hadn't been a monstrous error. "Now," I said firmly, though my cheeks burned as she stared at me. I'd imagined inspecting Leticia, of course, but in these daydreams I was invisible. I was shambling, bearlike; some years later I'd luck into a resemblance to Gerard Depardieu. But at that time, I suppose, he was an unknown French kid, also hoping to get laid.

I glanced at the clock over the door, where my mother had hung it when I started *preparatoria,* to encourage punctuality. "Never mind," I said. "The piano lesson finishes in half an hour."

"You don't know anything, do you?" Leticia said, smiling. She seemed to find the danger of the situation exciting. One minute before the bus would have stopped on the corner of Avenida Belgrano, we were back at the kitchen table, dressed and posed with the photo album. My mother walked in and greeted my new love politely, asked if she'd prefer tea or maté. As she turned to light the flame under the kettle, she said softly, "I'm sorry you're reduced to having sluts for friends, Peter."

Horrified, I turned to Leticia. The dark eyes I'd thought twenty minutes ago I was falling into were opaque; the smile on her pretty red lips didn't fade. She doesn't know German, I thought. She doesn't know anything, I thought. "Poor thing," I said.

Aliens

Because she has decided that it's the right thing to do, Sarah is baking cookies for her husband's girlfriend, Amy. Toll House cookies: who doesn't like them? Part of Sarah still thinks of chocolate chips as precious, like Lipton tea or Scotch tape. She lived the first nine years of her life in a slum outside Lima, Peru, where her parents were missionaries. It used to be that whenever the subject of South America came up at a dinner party, her husband, Paul, would say, "My wife is Peruvian, actually."

People would turn to Sarah, who's fair-skinned and blond, and tell her she didn't look Peruvian. She knew Paul was just trying to draw her into the conversation. She has a tendency to go quiet in company, to simply observe, as if she were invisible.

Maybe Peru is to blame for that. Certainly Sarah and her tow-headed little brothers weren't invisible there—they ran freely around Villa San Juan as if surrounded by a force field. This was before the Shining Path arrived and began executing anyone who could read. God was watching over them, her parents said. Well—God, and the American Embassy. Sarah and her brothers had blue eagle passports, along with their red Peruvian ones. They lived in a cinderblock house, like their neighbors, except theirs had a corrugated tin roof. Poor people's houses often were open to the sky in Lima, because it never rained. And though Sarah's family lived simply, like their neighbors, her mother kept valuable imports from Woolworth's in a metal trunk under the sink.

One day, Sarah used up a whole roll of Scotch tape, trying to hold together stones for a fort she and her friends were making. Her mother smacked her with a fly swatter—a common punishment in Villa San Juan, but not one that Sarah had experienced. She still remembers the row of children's puzzled faces peering into the bedroom window as she stroked her mother's hair. It was the parent, not the child, who was sobbing on the bed. Not long afterward, Sarah's family moved back to the States. She started fourth grade with a Spanish accent, long gone now.

Sarah measures brown and white sugar into a bowl; melts butter in the microwave. She works step by step, trying for consciousness, as her therapist has recommended. What she's conscious of is that she wants to be doing this when Julia and Miriam get home from school. She and Paul have agreed that this divorce and remarriage (if that's what it's going to be, and Sarah's pretty much given up the fantasy that Paul's going to come to the door one evening and say the whole thing with Amy was a crazy mistake) should disrupt their daughters' lives as little as possible. Paul's refused a promotion that would have kept him late at the office, so Sarah can continue teaching her English as a Second Language evening classes. The girls go to Paul's new apartment after an early supper; he provides dessert and brings them home at bedtime. The weekends Paul and Sarah divide.

Usually, when he drops them off on Sundays, he leans against the doorframe and he and Sarah chat about schoolwork, soccer practice. They report funny things their daughters have said, especially Miriam, who's eight. Sometimes Paul even teases Sarah—about how he smells bacon frying, for example. Now that there's nobody in the house who has to restrict salt and cholesterol, she and the girls eat bacon all the time. A person watching them who didn't know the situation might think that Paul was someone else's husband, jingling his car keys, harmlessly flirting.

Only once, since he moved out three months ago, has Amy's name been spoken between them. After the girls had gone upstairs, Paul complained that he'd heard that Sarah had told their friends that he'd met Amy online.

"I met her at a conference," he said.

"Well, you got to know her online," Sarah said, flushing. Absurdly, she was embarrassed at having been caught trying to make Paul sound worse than he is.

"E-mail. That's not at all the same thing. You make it sound like she was on some dating site."

Sarah said nothing.

"Amy wasn't looking for this, either," Paul said. "I know that probably makes no difference to you. But it wouldn't be right for the girls to hear this rumor, to think Amy's that kind of a person."

"What kind of a person is she?" Sarah said.

Paul looked as if he might cry. "A scientist." He turned and walked quickly to his car. Sarah watched him drive away, fast, without looking back, like Mel Gibson in an old movie she and the girls had watched recently, about aliens.

The real word for Amy is one from Sarah's childhood: adulteress. She remembers gazing at Mary Magdalene's picture in their children's Bible, trying to figure out what the pretty, red-haired woman had done. Amy, like Paul, does stem cell research. The lab where Paul works had received bomb threats, and that, Sarah had believed, was why Paul got a P.O. box. The true reason, she found out later, was so that Amy could send him packages, in addition to the e-mails. What could they have contained, she's often wondered—chocolates, used underwear, interesting lab samples?

She'd discovered the key in Paul's pants pocket. She didn't think anything of it. He'd seemed distracted lately, but she attributed this to the threats he faced at work. She dropped the key into a ceramic dish in the kitchen that holds items that may or may not find homes in the future: cup handles, pieces to board games, half-used rolls of cough drops.

A few days later, he found it. "Where was this?" Paul sounded both panicked and relieved.

"It fell out of those khakis. Is it important?"

"I thought I'd better get a box for my office mail."

"Because of the threatening letters?"

"Mmm-hmm."

Later, when everything else came out, Paul made a point of saying that that "Mmm-hmm" was the one time, in this whole mess, that he'd lied to her.

"If you could only hear yourself," Sarah said bitterly. She knew that for Paul, raised Catholic, this type of accounting mattered. He'd told her about going to confession, when it was still called that, and having to say how many times he'd been mean to his sister, how many times disrespectful to his parents, and being given a certain number of prayers to recite as punishment.

Religion, or rather, ex-religion, was what had brought them together, in college. They'd had the same freshman English teacher, a crotchety professor near retirement, who'd made everyone memorize a poem. Sarah and Paul both chose "Dover Beach." The Sea of Faith in the poem made Sarah think of the ocean near Lima, where nobody swam. The water was always gray and cold, reflecting the *garua* clouds that rolled into the city every morning, threateningly, yet never opened. Her parents said it was the fault of the Spanish Catholic priests: they'd forced the Indians to cut down all the trees and wrecked the climate.

When Sarah and Paul first became lovers, they joked

about sleeping with the enemy, because growing up he'd heard that Protestants were damned, especially Bible-thumping evangelicals. *AWOL Christian soldiers, marching off to bed,* Sarah sang softly, but Paul looked blank—Catholics don't learn hymns in Sunday school. What stays with you, leaving your religion, is the dread of doing the wrong thing; she and Paul both used to have that.

Shameless: more than one person has said this word to her, about Paul: the fact that he's shacked up with Amy just blocks from his old house. "Maybe he thinks he'll still have community pool privileges this summer," said one neighbor, darkly, who has power over who gets in.

Sarah knows Paul doesn't care about swimming. He'd take the girls and sit outside the fence, hot and shunned, if that was the Neighborhood Association's verdict. She knows he lives where he does because of his daughters; so they can skate or bike over to his place once the weather warms up. She knows that walking down their old street to the Metro station, having to greet people who used to think he was a great guy, is a wretched Calvary for him. But he does it, rather than take the long way around, which is what Amy probably does. Or maybe she works at a different lab, and drives; all Sarah knows is that she took whatever job she has and moved to suburban Washington, D.C. to be with Paul. What kind of woman would do that? Sarah thinks she's ready now to find out. She thinks the time has come to accept what she can't change, as Shelia, her therapist, who seems to have earned her degree by studying self-help best-sellers, keeps urging. So, cookies.

Sarah has the dry ingredients all lined up, ready to measure, when the girls come in through the back door. First eleven-year-old Julia, letting the storm door swing so that it whacks Miriam, following right behind, on the forehead. Miriam howls; more in anger than in pain, Sarah decides. She's going to let it go; she's going to stand here smiling, like Martha Stewart, brave, show-must-go-on Martha Stewart, with the cookie ingredients arranged in a row before her.

"What's that stuff for?" Julia says. Paul and Sarah hope Julia still doesn't realize how beautiful she is. She has Sarah's eyes and wavy hair; Paul's olive skin and fine bones. She's also an excellent student, and they want her to stay focused on that, and not think she can get by in life on her looks.

"Chocolate chip cookies," Sarah says brightly. "Hey, I make them all the time." Maybe not so much lately. Lately, what's on offer in this kitchen is bacon and English muffins and orange juice and gin. The four food groups of the abandoned, according to a divorced friend of Sarah's. "I thought I'd send some along with you girls for Amy," she says.

Julia lets her backpack fall straight from her shoulders to the floor. "Mom," she says, with a dramatic pause. "That is so totally whack."

"What's wacky about it? Doesn't Amy like cookies?" Sarah's heart pounds. She's never asked the girls a single question about Amy—her hair color, her age—not one thing.

"She does! I saw her eat one!" Miriam pipes up. Miriam, cuddly and naughty, is Sarah's favorite. Paul's favorite, too, which doesn't seem fair.

Sarah's mind begins spinning. Amy ate only one cookie, one time? Is she a dieter, who might influence Julia to develop an eating disorder? Paul deplores picky eaters; he likes a woman with an appetite. At least he always said he did. Maybe he's realized he prefers someone sleek and self-controlled: a scientist, sure.

Julia is still standing in the middle of the kitchen, breathing exasperatedly though her nose. "Mom, mom, mom, listen. What are you going to do? Go there and be like, 'I'm bummed you stole my husband Amy but I'm over it and so here are some cookies bye.'"

"Actually, yes," Sarah says slowly. "I wouldn't say I was over what happened between Daddy and me, but I think it's important to move in that direction." Heaven help her, she's talking like Shelia, the therapist.

"What I mean is, small gestures have significance, even when they seem crazy." Sarah feels on surer ground now—higher ground. "Look at those African-American students who sat at the lunch counters in the South. Many people thought that was crazy—and dangerous. People thought Grandma and Grandpa were crazy to raise three children in a poor village in Peru."

"Are you making the cookies to celebrate Martin Luther King?" Miriam says.

"In a way."

"I still say it's whack." Julia stomps upstairs. Julia's therapist says it's a good sign, the way she's challenging her mother. Sarah's beginning to think psychologists interpret pretty much any sign of life as a good one. The three of them go to shrinks who are out-of-network and terribly expensive, but Paul insists on paying for this. The offices are all in a building downtown Sarah had never noticed before. The Shrinking House, the girls call it; the Loony-Tunes Bin. Sarah has told them that attendance is not optional, so on Wednesdays they all pile in the car in clean clothes.

Julia says her therapist is a dolt. Sarah thinks she looks like Miriam, grown up: apple-cheeked; dressing in the kind of corduroy jumpers and colored tights Miriam favors. Miriam's therapist is pretty and young and wears dangly earrings, and now Miriam is campaigning to get her ears pierced. Then there's Sarah's therapist, Shelia, who tells her that she has a right to all her raging thoughts; that her desire to murder Amy is perfectly normal. This is helping her? Friends have advised her to find someone who's a better fit, as if Shelia were a pair of shoes. The very idea of dumping Shelia pains Sarah. She knows Shelia is trying hard. So she goes and sits there and waits for some illumination.

Miriam hangs her backpack up on its hook. "Can I help you, Mommy?" she says sweetly, ostentatiously Good, in contrast to Bad Julia.

Sarah checks the recipe one last time. It calls for baking soda and baking powder. If these cookies were for home consumption, she wouldn't bother, but she wants these to be perfect, so she fetches the can of baking powder from a top shelf. "We forgot this one very important thing. Do you want to measure it out, really carefully?"

Tongue clamped to the side of her mouth, Miriam levels off the measuring spoon with a knife, as Sarah taught her. Baking power sprinkles the counter, and she swirls her fingers in it and brings them to her lips.

"No, no, sweetheart. It's bitter." She wipes Miriam's hand with a dishtowel.

"I don't want to do this anymore."

"That's fine. You did a good job." Sarah's pleased it held her interest as long as it did. Miriam's short attention span and her intense craving for sweets are worrying. Her teachers have been hinting about putting her on medication, but Sarah and Paul have resisted. They hope, with therapy and extra tutoring, that Miriam can avoid drugs. One more reason, Sarah thinks, to form a bond with Amy: to enlist her help. As a scientist, she's probably good at problem solving, patient and methodical.

Quickly, she finishes up the cookies, fries bacon for BLT's, calls the girls to the table. Julia clomps downstairs, her sullen expression softening as she walks into the kitchen. Whose heart doesn't melt at the sight and smell of homemade cookies? She helps herself to one from the rack where they're cooling.

Miriam, already sitting at the kitchen table, screams. She jumps up and runs to her sister, bats the cookie out of her hand.

"Did you see what she did, Mom?" Julia cries. "God, what a brat."

"Don't say 'God,' please, Julia," Sarah sighs. "Miriam, we never hit. Sit. Down. Now."

Miriam obeys. "Don't eat any of Amy's cookies, Julia. Mommy and I put half a teaspoon of poison in them."

Half an hour later, the three of them are walking to Paul's new apartment, the cookies arranged nicely in an old Easter basket Sarah found in the basement. Julia refuses to carry it. "I don't want to walk through the neighborhood like some idiot Red Riding Hood."

"Little Red Riding Hood's mother should have poisoned the cake for the wolf, right?" Miriam says.

"Well, I don't know," Sarah smiles. "She didn't realize it was the wolf in the bed when she made the cake." Miriam's mistake is the kind of thing Paul would find funny. It will probably be some time, though, before they're all friendly enough for her to tell the story. "Anyway, poison's not very easy to buy."

"What about dishwashing powder?" Miriam says. She's been warned sternly, many times, not to taste it. Julia winks at her mother over Miriam's head, and Sarah feels a wash of gratitude—it's Julia's first friendly overture toward her in days.

It's a warm evening; one of the first in the year. Carlos, a Mexican gardener who works for several families in the neighborhood, is spreading mulch two doors down. Sarah greets him in Spanish and asks if his wife has had her baby yet. Middle-class life in America has become much more like middle-class life in Peru; almost everyone on their block has a Spanish-speaking servant: a cleaning woman, a nanny, a yardman. Sarah feels comfortable in this parallel universe: her first language was the unvarnished argot of poor people.

Once, last fall, a tall, handsome man with *Luis* stitched to the pocket flap of his Roto-Rooter shirt came to the door. Sarah was glad, because it seemed easier to describe the problem in Spanish. "Shit and pee are all over the basement floor," she told him.

"You sound Peruvian," Luis said wonderingly. His own speech contained the razor-crisp consonants of Lima's educated elite—the kind of accent that was mocked in Villa San Juan.

She explained. Luis looked respectful—missionaries get this, even from unbelievers. He told her he'd never been to Villa San Juan. "I would have been scared to go there," he said.

After he fixed the sewer pipe, he asked her for a glass of water. He drank it down standing in the kitchen. "Did you learn your profession in Peru?" Sarah said.

Luis gazed at her haughtily. "In Peru, I was a hydraulics engineer."

They spoke a few minutes more, about the political situation there. Then, as she held the door open for him he turned abruptly, took her hand and kissed the back of it.

The girls, doing their homework at the kitchen table,

couldn't wait to tell Paul. He was just home from a conference.

"Really? The plumber kissed Mommy?' he said, eyebrows raised, as Miriam danced around him, interrupting Julia.

"I think meeting a compatriot made him swoon," Sarah said, laughing. Lately, though, she's wondered whether Paul used this ridiculous incident to justify his own behavior.

Julia sighs, repeatedly and rudely, as Carlos narrates the harrowing delivery of his son. Sarah shoots her a warning look, and she edges away, trying to recruit Miriam in a hopping game. Miriam shakes her head and clings to Sarah.

"I must let you continue your walk in this pleasant weather," Carlos says. He probably knows exactly where they're going; the whole story of Paul's perfidy, although etiquette forbids any mention of the frailties of *los hombres*.

"Say *adios* to Carlos, girls," Sarah says. Miriam belts it out.

Julia hunches her shoulders and strides ahead, hands in the pockets of her jacket. "That was so embarrassing," she says.

"About the baby? It's just life, Julia. Everybody gets born."

"I mean it's embarrassing the way you're nicer to the maids and gardeners than to the regular people."

Righteous indignation seizes Sarah. "Who are you to say who the regular people are, missy?"

Julia's tall enough to meet her mother's gaze. "It's not us, that's for sure," she says. They've reached the point on the sidewalk in front of the apartment complex where Sarah usually leaves them. Paul's unit is off to the right, across the courtyard, and Julia stalks stiff-legged toward her father's new front door, with Miriam scampering behind. Sarah follows, holding the cookie basket.

Usually, she stays back, waiting on the sidewalk until the girls go inside, and she's never been able to see who opens the door. She doesn't even know if Amy's home when the girls arrive.

Now, here's a woman who must be Amy, holding the door ajar. The girls rush in past her like a pair of dogs. Sarah freezes, clutching the basket of cookies.

I almost died, people say. That's what it feels like: a mortification so massive that she hears a roaring in her ears. What insanity possessed her, believing cookies would be a good idea? Absolutely, absolutely, it was wrong, she thinks.

At the same time, she sizes Amy up. She's about Sarah's height; her shoulder-length hair is light brown. It looks like hair that doesn't go frizzy in humidity. She's wearing a scarlet wool coat that Sarah remembers considering in a mail order catalogue before settling on the more practical navy.

"Just some cookies," Sarah says, holding out the ludicrous offering, which, she now sees, has a row of rabbits stenciled along the base. They appear to be cavorting in obscene positions. How on earth could she have ended up owning this thing? She's like the fruit vendors in Lima, sweet old ladies obliviously wearing secondhand T-shirts with English inscriptions like "Hot Babe."

Amy takes the proffered basket. She, too, looks like she

might pass out. Sarah wonders whether Paul has told this woman that his wife is dead, or in a mental hospital.

"So Julia gets her curly hair from you," Amy says finally.

"Oh, yes." Sarah turns and walks quickly back down the brick walk.

She realizes that what Paul has told Amy about his wife is that she's Peruvian. What Amy must have pictured was a woman across a vast cultural chasm: in a woolly cap with ear flaps, maybe, wearing dozens of petticoats, leading a llama. A woman who's never felt quite at home in this country; who returns in dreams to the dusty village of her birth, where she scampers to the cliffs with her brothers to look at the ocean.

Head down, purse tucked under her arm, Sarah starts running home. Dressed in the tweed skirt and sweater she wears for teaching, she feels as though she's truly *running—* away from flood, fire, wild animals, the way humans evolved to do. But her unusual exercise-wear seems to have alarmed some passer-by, because she hears a car slow down behind her. It pulls over next to the curb.

"Sarah!" It's Paul's voice. She stops and turns around.

"What on earth?" he cries. "I'm sitting at my desk when Julia bursts in saying that you've gone crazy. Then here's Miriam saying you've baked poisoned cookies, followed by Amy, crying her eyes out with this bizarre pornographic basket."

"You have a desk there?" Sarah says. Oddly, a desk at his girlfriend's place seems like a bigger betrayal than a bed.

"It's from Ikea," he says.

Sarah rests a hand against the rough trunk of a silver maple, still breathing hard. "Tell me one thing, Paul. And tell me the truth, for a change. Did you say to Amy, back in the beginning, that I was Peruvian?"

"I don't discuss you with Amy."

"Did you say I was Peruvian?"

"I don't—well, maybe. I can't remember everything I've ever said." He looks at her worriedly. "Sarah, what's wrong with you?"

She rushes at him; hits him, hard, on the shoulder. She hits him again in the chest. Then she covers her face with her hands and bursts into tears.

Paul puts his arm around her. "Come on; I'll drive you home."

In the car, her tears cease instantly, as if she were Miriam bribed with a treat. "Well," she says briskly. "I suppose the neighbors will change their minds about who's at fault, after my little performance."

Paul looks at her sidelong. "They won't—I'm still the shit." He says this calmly. He's never tried to dodge blame, to shirk responsibility. The divorce terms he's offered her are more than fair.

They're home. Sarah looks up at the small brick house, which seemed baronial when they bought it ten years ago. Someone they knew, who'd made an internet fortune, named his mansion after the cedars along the drive, and Paul and Sarah took to calling their house after the changing situation in the yard: "The Lone Tulip." "The Virginia Creeper." "The Dead Hostas."

"*The world which seemed to lie before us like a land of dreams,*" Sarah says.

"I don't think I could recite that poem now if you held a gun to my head," Paul says.

"I have no immediate plans to do that," Sarah says.

Paul cuts the motor. His expression, when he turns to her, is full of concern. "Are you sure you wouldn't like me to come in for a while? You don't seem quite yourself."

Even in their worst moments, they've shown consideration for each other; civility. Sheila has suggested that all this niceness might have been part of their problem. And yet, isn't it a good thing to fall back on, when everything else is ashes?

"I'm all right," Sarah says. Is she? She's light-headed, as though she's run for miles in a high altitude. Coca leaves were the Peruvian remedy for that. The enslaved Indians chewed them in order not feel hunger and cold; coca-leaf tea is still prescribed for every ailment: stomach-ache, fevers, grief. Sarah and her brothers joke that they drank so much of it as children they'd still probably flunk a drug test. "You'd better get back, Paul."

It's the relief that washes over his face as he starts the car that ignites something within her—his evident satisfaction at having, once again, done the right thing. Smugly confessing sin, Paul has transferred his faith from God to himself. It's only Sarah, then, who's been wandering in the wilderness.

"Go to hell," she says softly.

"Sorry?"

She imagines that he can't *see* her, either—marching smartly up the steps to the front door that's now entirely her own. She unlocks it; enveloped in clouds, surrounded by a force field, alien, invisible.

Do Not Call

It was the dark, dark fourth year of the millennium when Helen had an affair. Suddenly, it seemed, nobody was thinking rationally any more—there'd been talk of having delivery people watch for suspicious activity along their routes and report it to Homeland Security.

"Oh, no!" she exclaimed, peering through the miniblinds as footsteps scraped up the front walk. Her lover, Tom, sat up, wild-eyed, clutching the sheets. Helen had assured him her husband was out of town. "It's…FedEx!"

Tom laughed, a little breathlessly. "You're mad," he said, and kissed her and kissed her with relief. "A mad housewife."

Tom was twenty-five, with curly black hair and a Roman nose. His skin hadn't completely cleared up. Helen was only seven years older, but it seemed like more, to both of them.

Her name was on the deed of a brick house and she was the mother of a twelve-year-old.

Helen's husband was Pedro Roth, the Argentinean playwright. She'd met him while she was still in college, a romance that just skirted the edge of scandal—he wasn't her professor, and she didn't get pregnant until after she'd completed her honors thesis on Latin American drama. She'd thrown up at the commencement party, having sat for two hours in the sun in black robes, but she wasn't the only one of her classmates to do so. Dancing with a boy from her freshman dorm, she'd put one hand over her still-secret belly and felt something turn over, slowly, like a wad of wet clothes in a dryer.

"Great sinsemilla, isn't it," the boy said, mistaking her beatific smile.

Marrying Pedro had seemed fated, not least because her Quaker parents had once sent a letter urging the Argentinean military government to free him from prison. The outcome they hadn't imagined was to have him sitting on their sofa in Philadelphia, gazing hungrily at their only child as he scratched the schnauzer's ears. Helen had previously intended to join the Peace Corps. She, who never made her bed, was to have taught village women to boil drinking water and plant nutritious vegetables.

Instead, she moved to Washington with Pedro in August. Under her extra-large t-shirts, her baby was a basketball that radiated heat. Women Pedro had known in Argentina sat smoking in their tiny Georgetown apartment, praising the way Helen's arms and legs and face stayed slender.

"How can they bear to talk about thinness?" she cried, at night as Pedro curled around her like a shell. Some of the women had been political prisoners during the dictatorship; one, in hiding, had scavenged food from hotel bins in Mar del Plata.

"Reality keeps turning the page," Pedro said, quoting himself.

Certainly Helen wasn't what he'd been raised to expect in a wife. After their son, Joaquin, was born, he'd come home to a wall-to-wall mess that caused a flicker of despair to cross his face before he'd tuck a tea towel into his belt and start gathering up the toys and diapers. Years later, he told her he'd never seen a man in Argentina hold a baby except to pose for a photograph.

A dozen years later, in the Maryland suburbs, Helen was a crack housekeeper. Her house was tidy and smelled nice; there were vases of fresh flowers. One late summer day, when Pedro was in Miami with Joaquin, Helen invited Tom over. It was four in the afternoon—the old playdate hour. And suddenly, her comfy red sofa, her Peruvian rugs with parrots and llamas on them, the green apples in a yellow bowl, all seemed to her to be products of a child's aesthetic imagination.

"I've never slept with a woman who owned a washer-dryer," Tom said, standing in her kitchen in hiking boots.

They both edited newsletters—hers on family planning, his on gay rights—which was how they'd met.

"Do you want to do your laundry?" Helen asked. When he appeared to hesitate, she said swiftly, "I'm kidding."

"I knew that," Tom said. He turned and clumped up the stairs as if he knew where her bedroom was, though their previous encounters had taken place at his apartment in Adams Morgan. He examined the pictures on her dresser with his hands behind his back, wearing a respectful expression like someone touring Mount Vernon.

Helen opened her closet and took out a blouse she planned to change into later.

"That's pretty," Tom said. Maybe he understood that she was stalling, avoiding this final Rubicon which was her own bed. Then she swept all her shirts off their hangers and tossed them one by one onto the duvet. She folded her arms and looked at him.

"I don't get it," Tom said.

"I know a guy who used to tell women he wrote for the *New Republic* on a first date," Helen said. "If the woman said, 'Which republic is that?' he didn't call her again."

"Well, how can I weep into your shirts without wrinkling them?" Tom said. "Old Sport."

Helen laughed and started unbuttoning her jeans.

"I'm used to being thought dumb at work," Tom said. "Everyone's really nice to me and pleased to have a straight guy in the office, but I'm always having to prove I'm not dumb."

"I guess that was mean of me," Helen said. She resolved to be nicer to him, but then, half an hour later, she teased him with the FedEx man.

"You know what I think?" Tom said, when he'd finally recovered his breath. "I think you're tired of me."

Helen smiled and said nothing.

He called a couple of times after that afternoon; she made excuses. But then, to her dismay, he kept calling. Usually in the afternoon. between the time she ferried Joaquin to soccer practice and guitar lessons and picked up the dry cleaning and a plastic-wrapped dead animal for dinner (Joaquin was trying, unsuccessfully so far, to persuade his parents to become vegetarians).

"Can't we at least talk?" Tom would say.

Helen's heart would skid, as if on an area rug. "Thank you, but we're not interested," she'd say, and hang up. The little hitch in her voice was identical, she believed, to the controlled irritation with which she handled the dozen or so telemarketers who also called.

"We need caller I.D., Mom," Joaquin said, looking up from his third after-school bowl of cereal. He wanted them to dine on plants like their hominid ancestors, but he also required things like broadband, MP3, CD burners, to survive. Most computer words sounded harsh and totalitarian to Helen.

"I signed up for that Do Not Call list," she said. "When it goes into effect, the telemarketers are supposed to stop."

Whenever Joaquin was near the phone, he'd lunge for it and try to keep the telemarketer on the line, asking silly questions. Helen was surprised by how often he succeeded—his voice was still that of a child. But even though he was toying with people who must have taken those awful jobs out of desperation (she'd tried to impress this upon him) he seemed hurt when they hung up on him.

"That one didn't even give me a chance," he'd say mournfully.

That one must have been Tom, Helen would think. He always hung up when Joaquin answered. And he never called after seven, when Helen's husband was likely to be home. The very idea of Pedro Roth had always seemed to intimidate him. He'd read Pedro's classic play, *Into a Million Pieces*, in college.

"Does your husband know about me?" he'd asked her once.

"Of course not." They were on Tom's bed, which was a mattress on a floor under a window. The conversations wafting in from the street were Spanish—the language, for Helen, of love and secrets.

"What do you think he'd do if he found out?"

She shook her head. "I've never done this before."

"You're kidding!" Tom cried, delightedly. "Actually, I've never been with a married woman, either. Marina dated one for a while, though. It was kind of a disaster."

Marina was Tom's roommate. Tom's brother, who was also gay, had been living with them, too, but recently he'd followed a man he was in love with to California.

"You didn't tell her about us, did you?" Helen said, feeling a wash of fear. Books and movies often portrayed this adulterous terror as a thrill. But she didn't care for amusement park rides, either.

"Don't worry," Tom said. "Marina's never heard of your husband."

In Tom's kitchen, the fridge was covered with pictures of himself and his brother and Marina in three-musketeer poses. Marina was blonde and cheerleader-cute. Other photos showed her with a girlfriend, who did look gay, Helen thought: thin and sad-eyed. She decided the reason Marina didn't was that she smiled like someone who'd never been oppressed a day in her life.

Helen turned from the pictures back to Tom, who was slicing a lemon to put into a glass of ice water she'd asked for. "Someday you're going to make some lucky girl very happy," she said, in an old-lady voice.

"When?" Tom said. "When can I see you again?"

They both had flexible schedules. They liased with likeminded people in likeminded organizations. Regime change in America: that was the overarching goal. If they'd been Argentineans, twenty years earlier, they might have been arrested, flown up in military planes, and pushed, alive, into the sea. Helen's husband had known someone this had happened to, in Buenos Aires. As for Pedro, he'd been lucky not to have been tortured to death before Amnesty kicked up such a fuss—his captors had told him so when they released him. Now *Into a Million Pieces* was part of the antiwar canon, like *Catch-22* and *All Quiet on the Western Front.*

A few months earlier, however, Pedro had shocked Helen by announcing that he was in favor of the invasion of Iraq. "If America had invaded during our dictatorship, maybe twenty-five thousand people wouldn't have disappeared," he'd said.

"Invaded how? Shock and awe over Buenos Aires?"

"If that was what was necessary."

"But then the political prisoners would have died anyway! You might have died!"

Pedro shrugged. "I've sometimes wished it had been so."

Helen stared at him, aghast. "Wished or wish?"

"Both, actually."

Tears sprang to her eyes. From the time she'd first known him, Pedro had told her that she, Helen, had saved his life. She didn't know how she'd done it; it was like hearing about a heroic deed you'd performed when you were an infant, or asleep. But over the years, she'd come to accept it as true. Though his plays were grim and bleak, interviewers frequently noted how cheerful he was in person. "I have a happy marriage, a happy family; how could I not be cheerful?" was his reply.

Pedro was no different in private. He was never in a bad mood—he opened his eyes every morning and smiled at the sight of her. And he doted on Joaquin, attending his son's soccer games in a jacket and tie like the dapper South American gentleman he was—he was only fifty, but that was older in Argentina than it was in America.

Now he put his arms around her and kissed her hair. "Please don't cry, *mi amor.* It's simply the truth."

The truth, which to Helen had always sounded like *the blue*—a wide, free expanse of sky—suddenly revealed itself to be a dark, sharp-clawed creature that had tunneled its way into her ribcage.

There it stayed, though Pedro acted like he'd forgotten what he'd said. Or maybe he thought it was no big deal, to tell your wife you'd just as soon have died before ever laying eyes on her. He'd come home in the evenings and pour two glasses of Argentinean wine and they'd sit out on the screened porch in the deepening spring twilight and talk, as they always had—about Joaquin, the events of the day, the minutiae of running a household.

Pedro fretted about his new play, which was scheduled to open in Miami next fall. He thought the young director didn't understand it, even in translation.

"Maybe an American director can't imagine what your characters endured," Helen said. When she was first getting to know Pedro, she'd tried to imagine it. He wouldn't tell her much, so she'd started reading a book called *Nunca Más,* about torture under the Argentinean military. But she'd had to stop after a couple of pages—she'd felt sick to her stomach. For years, she'd been haunted by those few pages.

"If he can't imagine, then I have failed," Pedro said. He

looked gloomy for a moment, then met her eyes and smiled. "Meanwhile I've become a real American, haven't I, talking obsessively of work. Soon I'll be one of those people hunched over a blueberry."

"I think you mean a Blackberry," Helen said.

He laughed, enjoying his mistake. "The Fruits of Labor— that sounds like a title for something. But *querida*, tell me about your day."

He was unfailingly like this—courtly, considerate. He listened attentively as Helen described a lunch she'd attended with the editors of a gay rights newsletter. But she didn't tell Pedro about the young man she'd met, who was devoting himself to the cause not because he was gay but because he loved his brother. It was the kind of story Pedro would have liked hearing, and there was no reason to avoid mentioning Tom. All Helen had done, so far, was have coffee with him after the luncheon. Yet she didn't mention him.

Nor did they discuss the war. The President had recently landed on an aircraft carrier and declared the mission accomplished. But maybe Pedro agreed with that, thinking of the thousands whose memories of torture, unlike his, had been wiped away forever.

Helen didn't know what he thought, and now she wondered if she ever had. She'd always attributed the slightly formal way he treated her to his being so much older, and Argentinean. But now his Old World manners, which her friends had always swooned over, seemed to her false and hollow. It would be better, she thought, if he came home and lay on the sofa in front of the TV, like a normal husband.

I'm married to this foreign old man, she told herself, coldly, when they were making love. The way her body responded was its own business; she, Helen, wasn't there.

Here is where she was, one hot afternoon in early June: in a dark, chilly restaurant off Dupont Circle. She was peeling foil from the neck of a bottle of beer and rolling the bits between her fingers. Helen wasn't used to drinking at noon, and neither, apparently, was Tom, whom she'd called and invited to lunch.

They'd spent the previous hour deploring: judges pawing over women's medical records, the administration's determination to keep homosexuals from marrying. Then Tom said abruptly, "All this time what I've really been thinking is how I'd like to go to bed with you."

Helen laughed. "So you're actually not in favor of gay marriage or reproductive choice for women?"

"I bet you get hit on all the time," Tom said. He looked down at his unfinished steak frites. It had pleased her that when she'd told him it was her treat he hadn't ordered the cheapest thing.

"Not really," Helen said. She giggled again. That seemed so dotty she felt compelled to explain: "My husband recently told me about a friend of his who'd gotten fired for hitting women up."

Tom smiled politely. "Forgive me. You're happily married."

"Uh-huh. We mostly argue over prepositions."

She shook hands with Tom in the blinding sunshine outside the restaurant and scurried home, where she embarked on a complicated, many-stepped recipe for dinner. She realized that she'd neglected the house, too, lately—the window screens weren't up, and here it was, almost summer. Pedro claimed to forget such tasks because the seasons here were opposite to those in South America.

She was struggling to lock a sash in place when Joaquin walked in. "Mom, why can't I have a cell phone?" This was the opening gambit of a debate which he picked up daily, like a long-running chess game.

"Because your father and I said you could have one when you're thirteen," Helen said.

"But why can't I have one now?"

"Because you're not thirteen yet."

"Dad has one. We could get a two-for-one deal and then we'd all three have phones."

"I don't want a cell phone. And you may have one when you're thirteen." Suddenly, the sash cord broke and the window smashed down on Helen's hand. She cried out.

"Why not now, Mom?"

Helen whirled around, clutching her throbbing fingers. "What's the matter with you guys? Can't you see I'm hurt?"

"Us guys?" Joaquin looked puzzled. "Sorry—I didn't realize," he said, gazing at her with his father's mild, alien eyes.

* * *

She saw Tom again a couple of days later, squinting into the sun at a bus stop on Connecticut Avenue, and pulled over to offer him a ride. He didn't even pretend not to stare at her bare arms, at her braless summer dress.

"Muslim clerics are probably right about burqas," Helen said.

"Probably," Tom said.

"Is your car in the shop?"

"It's in San Francisco with my brother."

"My husband doesn't drive, either." That *either* was, in retrospect, significant. So was the open parking space in front of Tom's building, miraculous as an oasis. Helen followed him up three flights of gray-carpeted stairs, into a dusty, sunlit living room that had the anonymous disorder of a dorm lounge.

"Where's that ice water you promised?" Helen said—that was the ostensible reason she'd squeezed into a parallel space and climbed the stairs. Tom stood behind her and put his arms around her and they swayed as if to music. Maybe because the apartment recalled her college days, stumbling mouth to mouth with this boy toward a bed strewn with damp towels and dirty socks didn't feel as momentous as she'd imagined. Instead, she seemed to have stepped back in time and found herself in a room she'd forgotten, the way you did in dreams.

Helen remembered marveling, as a teenager, that everyone, in every country of the world, figured sex out, the very

45

mechanics seemed so implausible. They still sort of did, and yet, because of them, she careened home across the city, listening moonily to one of Joaquin's pop music stations, where the song lyrics struck her suddenly as profound.

Ice water became the codeword. Tom would call her at her office and suggest it. The dark, clawed creature lodged inside Helen's ribcage began melting, melting, like the wicked witch. Yet it was when she was driving away from Tom, through the white-hot, shimmering streets, that she felt happy, not when she was with him. When she was with him, she was impatient and irritable.

"Don't play with that, please," she snapped at him once, as he fiddled with her car cigarette lighter.

"Yes, *Mother*," Tom said, and Helen flushed. Then she saw, out of the corner of her eye, that he'd lit a cigarette. He smoked after sex—a predictable affectation of young leftists, she'd told him.

"Of all the nerve—smoking in my car!" She was glad he was showing nerve, though. His deference to her made her hate herself.

"Doesn't your husband smoke?" Tom said. "He's smoking on his book jacket."

"That's an old picture. He says prison was a good place to quit."

"Whoa. I guess so," Tom said. He took a deep drag and tossed the cigarette out the window.

When she picked Pedro up later that evening he said, "Who's been smoking?"

"Someone I met from the gay and lesbian newsletter."

"Did you know that smoking in a person's car is a sign of sexual attraction?" Pedro said. He looked at her sidelong. "Better be careful around her."

"I don't think I'm in danger of falling for a lesbian."

"Maybe she's in danger of falling for you, though."

"Yessir, that's me," Helen said. For some unfathomable reason, she was speaking in a hillbilly accent. "A real femme fatale."

She'd never been a femme fatale. But Pedro, in his youth, had been a *mujeriego,* a womanizer. The Argentinean women who'd hung out that summer in their Georgetown apartment had told her stories, laughing. She'd understood even then that they'd only meant to illustrate how he'd changed. And it wasn't freedom and coming to America that had done it, the women insisted. It was Helen.

Pregnant, she'd stare at her pale, oily face in the mirror and wonder. It was a young face, certainly, but not one that could have launched a thousand ships.

Once, driving in her car with Tom, with the music blaring, Helen glanced over at the driver in the next lane and recognized a woman she knew, a neighbor. There was nothing to do but smile and wave and drive on.

Later, in line at Giant, she heard a low chuckle behind her: "Busted!"

Helen turned around and beamed at her neighbor. "Don't I wish. He's from the Gay and Lesbian Campaign." The woman snapped her fingers. "Oh, the irony."

Her dread of discovery subsided a little: Pedro was flying frequently down to Miami to monitor the progress of his play. She continued to worry that Joaquin would find out, though, and be damaged; she'd read a novel in which a teenager sleuthed out his mother's infidelity. But gradually she realized that her son wasn't interested in spying on her—he was more concerned with her not spying on him. He considered himself a teenager already, and spent his summer days with his friends, swooping on their bikes like a flock of bats in the driveway of the neighborhood's prettiest girl. The changes he noted in Helen, such as her improved taste in car radio stations, he seemed to attribute to his influence.

"Your hair looks much better long, Mom," he said, shaking his own shoulder-length locks.

"I see the heat and humidity are agreeing with you," Pedro told her. "How about a trip to Miami next week?"

"In August? No thank you. But I know a twelve-year-old who'd give his eye teeth."

After she dropped Pedro and Joaquin at the airport, she called Tom and invited him over. She could have spent the whole week with him, danced every night away, but instead she sent him away after an hour, with a Ziploc bag of cookies, like a brisk, motherly prostitute.

"What 'stuff' do you have to do?" he pleaded, lingering by the front door.

"Open the box I just got from Lands' End, obviously. There—" she kissed him almost viciously. "Go!"

She cleaned the whole house furiously, as if he'd left great, muddy footprints everywhere.

Tom's unwanted phone calls continued for a few weeks, then stopped. After the Do Not Call law passed, the telemarketing calls stopped, too. In the evenings, at dinner, there was quiet.

"It kind of renews your faith," Helen said. "I don't know in what, exactly, but it renews your faith."

It had been three months since she'd last seen Tom. Helen knew that she'd come close to ruining her life, and this near miss made her grateful to him; if he'd chosen to he could have been her undoing. She felt guilty, in a humming, low-grade way, about how she'd used him to repair her marriage and then tossed him away. Although maybe he'd used her, too—think of the time she'd saved him, last summer, waiting for buses on steamy sidewalks.

"Here's to the renewed faith of atheists," Pedro said, raising his glass.

"What about those poor people who took telemarketing jobs out of desperation?" Joaquin said. He was wolfing his pork chops in order to go meet his friends at the mall. Three months ago, he was a vegetarian who scorned shopping. Wait a darn minute here, Helen wanted to say. Time out. Instead she skittered after him like an old babushka, urging a scarf, extra money for emergency.

"A cell phone would be better than money, in an emergency," Joaquin said, grinning. But he pocketed the twenty she held out, and vanished.

Helen plopped down on the sofa with a weary sigh, as if she'd been chasing a toddler all day. "At last, alone," Pedro said, in the Latin-lover voice he did to make her laugh. He sat down next to her and took her face in his hands.

The phone, which wasn't supposed to bother them any more, did. But they couldn't just let it ring, with their child out in the dark. Was the terror alert yellow or orange?

Pedro answered. "May I ask what this is concerning?" He handed the receiver to Helen with a look she couldn't translate. "A Marina."

"Oh, hi, Marina! How are you guys?" Helen burbled, though she'd never actually met Tom's roommate.

"Bitch. You really hurt Tom."

"Oh."

There was more—a whole sewer backup. Helen was shocked by the things Tom had revealed to Marina about her; private things she'd said and done. "Tom doesn't know I called," Marina said. "This is just me, avenging."

"I understand," Helen said, and hung up.

"That's what that Marina person told me," Pedro said, from the armchair he'd moved to, across the room. He hadn't turned the lamp on.

"What?"

"She said you'd understand why she was calling."

"Yes." It crossed Helen's mind that Marina might be in love with Tom. What else could explain that kind of fury? She put her face in her hands and burst into tears.

"So she did fall for you," Pedro said, his voice cold and severe. "Did you imagine, if it wasn't another man, that I wouldn't be jealous?"

"What you'd feel had nothing to do with it, Pedro."

He made a sound that could have been pain or its opposite. It was the wordlessness of it that broke her heart. She'd pulled him to safety and then loosened her grip, letting him slide toward the abyss. "I want to tell you the whole truth," she said at last.

"Absolutely not. I forbid it."

"Forbid—what kind of talk is this?"

"I don't want to know. Keep it to yourself." He stood and walked out of the room.

Helen realized that she'd never experienced Pedro's anger before; what she'd thought was anger, in the past, was merely irritation. In a strange way it reassured her: that he turned his back to her in bed; that he only spoke to her when civility required it. She felt as though she'd gotten up in darkness and at last put her hand out and touched a wall.

"Are you and Dad fighting again?" Joaquin asked her, after a week of this.

"Again?" Helen said. "When in all your life before have we fought?"

He shrugged. "It makes it seem more normal if I say that."

Pedro flew down to Miami for the premiere of his play and didn't even suggest that she accompany him. He didn't call her, and he never answered his cell phone, though it would have been like him to forget it on the plane, or in his suitcase. Days passed, and she wondered if she should call the police, or a divorce lawyer. She called Tom, and heard his voice give a message that was new: *Marina and Tom can't come to the phone right now...*

She called back again and again, trying to determine the degree of tenderness with which he said their two names. After the seventh call, she remembered that Tom had caller ID. She sat with her hand on the receiver, breathless with embarrassment, and in this fugue of mortification was able to muster the courage to call Pedro once more. He answered in Spanish.

"How's the play?" she said.

"*Bien.*"

In the background of wherever he was, she heard tango music and gusts of laughter. A cast party, she thought. But maybe not—maybe he'd already left her, and she was hearing the first sounds of his new life. She took a deep breath. "And that director you thought was all wrong?"

"Him! To my astonishment, Helen—"

Pedro plunged, as into a pool, into a description of the actors, the actresses, the sets, the lighting, how certain lines had gone over. He had a tendency, like Joaquin, to tell her every blessed minute of a show that impressed him.

"I miss you so," she said.

"*Díos mío*," Pedro said. "Without you is unendurable."

"Sure you don't want to go with me to meet Dad at the airport?" Helen said later that night, standing in the doorway of Joaquin's room.

He turned to look at her, his computer screen glowing behind him. "Nah." Maybe he noticed her earrings, lipstick, perfume, and guessed that she wanted to go alone. More likely, he savored the prospect of even brief freedom. "You'll be back in what, an hour?"

"Right, so be good."

"Right." Joaquin smiled indulgently. "Don't forget your cell phone." He'd gotten one, too—he'd prevailed in the end, as children always will. Soon, judging from the size of his St. Bernard-puppy feet, he'd tower over his parents.

Thirteen years ago, Joaquin had been the urgent reason Helen and Pedro had gotten married. And yet her pregnancy had been a pretext—proof of the unlikely connection between a man who'd seen what hell was like and a college girl who'd scarcely heard voices raised in anger.

Her car glided past the bare trees along the parkway toward the river, around the great stone monuments that floated, golden and unreal, in the darkness. Over the past week winter cold had set in, and a watery crust of snow lay over Washington—Pedro was arriving from a place of sun and Latin warmth. Often, it seemed to Helen, meeting Pedro amounted to a collision of weather fronts, atmospheres— even at the end of an ordinary workday: *You? Me? In America? Ah, yes.* Then he would smile, and remember.

And now? She guessed he'd have forgotten to bring a coat; a spare down jacket was piled on the seat beside her, her new silver cell phone in its folds. Suddenly, the little phone began to glow and clamor, but when Helen reached for it, the thing slithered over the nylon of the jacket and under the passenger seat, where it rang, seemingly plaintively, and went silent. One more piece of technology aimed at making you frantic! But she couldn't stop to look for it—all along the terminal, police cars were parked at angles, lights flashing, telling everyone to keep moving, that these were new, perilous times.

When Pedro was released from prison, in Argentina, he'd been driven out of Buenos Aires in a car trunk and left in the countryside, to walk back through bare winter fields. "All night, I had two things," he'd told the uncomprehending, twenty-year-old Helen. "I was alive, and anyone I'd last seen alive still could be."

Now she understood: that hope not only clung to threads but made a nest of them and raised offspring. She circled the airport and looped back toward the glassy cliff of the terminal. Finally, beyond the long line of cars, she spotted Pedro on the sidewalk in shirtsleeves, his breath streaming out in white clouds. He turned and saw her. She inched forward, heart pounding, in perfect, companionable silence.

Flames

In fourth grade Joaquin Roth and I were still officially best friends, but I was losing him. He'd play Sims with me only if there was nothing else to do—putting a toilet in the living room and gasoline in the swimming pool. "That's life," he'd say, shrugging, when our characters went swimming and were trapped by flames.

"He's a nine-year-old boy, Edith," Mrs. Roth said, stroking my hair as I wept into their corduroy sofa cushions. "You can't expect so much." She showed me the letter she'd gotten about her ancestor, Thomas Jefferson. She was excited because she'd just found out she's part African-American, though she's pale and blonde.

The weekend she went to the Jefferson family reunion was the last time Joaquin slept over. When Mrs. Roth dropped him off, my mother said, with a laugh, "Pretty soon we're not going to allow this." I didn't know what was funny, because my life so far had taught me that the older you got, the more you were allowed to do.

So seven years later, I get it. My boyfriend Sam's mother even quit her job over me. She said she didn't want him coming home to an empty house—though, as Sam said, it was hardly empty with me in it. Once we tried doing it against the back wall of the library, a position he'd seen in a French movie. But the bricks were scraping me and I didn't know what to do with my legs. It was like a failed physics experiment—it didn't work to stand, but I couldn't wrap my legs around him, either. "You're not exactly a lightweight," Sam said, and I started laughing, and that was the end of that. All the way home he kept apologizing, saying it had been completely different in the movie.

"Oh, for Pete's sake," I said. I have my dead grandmother's name, and when I'm exasperated I seem to channel her. "Haven't you heard of this thing called special effects?"

Joaquin and Sam play soccer together, and this fall they became friends. This is how you can tell if two guys are friends: one of them will fart, and the other will laugh and call him gay. If they're enemies, same thing, except nothing is said about gayness because that would be bullying. Here in Maryland there's a lot of respect for your sexual orientation, which is good, because in addition to Sam, I was somewhat in love with Mrs. Roth and with Joaquin's girlfriend, Julia.

Julia was new this year and noticed at once how beautiful Joaquin is. The rest of us were used to it; plus, he hates anyone mentioning his looks, because it's gay to be too handsome. You can say that about yourself since it's self-deprecating.

In the hallway, Julia said to no one in particular, as if she were in a documentary about herself, "Joaquin Roth looks exactly like John Mayer."

"His dad does even more," I said, stepping up next to her. "That is, he used to, in his book-jacket picture. He's a famous writer from Argentina. He was a political prisoner who was tortured, and when Joaquin's mom was in high school, she signed a letter about him for Amnesty International. Then later she met him and got pregnant. It's a pretty amazing coincidence that she saved his life."

I didn't mean to say all that when I opened my mouth. But in a way, I was promoting Mr. Roth's books.

Julia looked me over then, and it was as if I could see her brain click "refresh." In my favor, I have clear skin and eyes the color of good bourbon. My dad says I'm not fat—I'm a force of nature. Julia is tall and slim and has wavy hair and long lashes. She could be Joaquin's twin sister, and it was almost as if they became a couple by popular acclaim.

So, after seven years I was hanging out at the Roths' again. At first I was nervous about going inside, but Joaquin said his parents never blamed me for what happened after the sleepover. I was standing in their entryway, inhaling the Roth smell—lemon soap, old books, garlic, some kind of Argentinean aftershave—amazed at how their furniture had shrunk. "The prodigal daughter returns!" Mrs. Roth exclaimed, hugging me. She felt even thinner than my mother. I asked her how the Jefferson family reunion had gone.

"We're all Facebook friends now," she said. "Isn't that incredible?" To an adult it was, obviously. Julia snickered, and I hoped she would be nice to Mrs. Roth, who has had breast cancer.

What happened seven years ago was that kids at school found out Joaquin was staying at our house, and by the end of recess, rumors were flying. We were "sleeping together." I was an "easy lay." We were "shtupping." It got worse. Fourthgraders have terrible potty mouths, though even the doctors' kids didn't completely know what they were saying. Joaquin and I walked home separately, and then he went up to our guest room and packed his suitcase and dragged it the four blocks to his house. I'm not sure why I followed him. It was as if the disgusting things the kids had said were true, and I was helplessly connected to him.

Mr. Roth was home, but upstairs writing in his study. Joaquin had been staying with us because in Argentina fathers aren't very hands-on with their kids. Although now he's at every soccer game in a jacket and tie, as if it were a piano recital.

The first thing Joaquin did when he let himself into the house was to start fixing a snack of ramen. I'd taught him how to do this, how to slice a carrot into coins while the noodles boil. I was standing outside the Roths' house at the kitchen window, watching Joaquin as if he were on a cooking show directed by me, and the misery of the school day began to fade. Then he went to tip the carrot pieces into the pan, and the flannel sleeve of his shirt dangled into the flame. I screamed, and unlike with TV, Joaquin heard me. He whirled around, and the flame got bigger. I ran inside, and pretty soon I was on fire, too.

The next year in school we read *Johnny Tremain*. I read it twice, it was so good.

One day I happened to be standing behind Joaquin in the cafeteria line, close enough to smell the oily, doggy smell of his hair. It was a little gross, but it also made me want to bury my nose in it. We hadn't really spoken since the fire. My parents had sued his—not because they hated the Roths, my mother explained, but because of the insurance. But they didn't want me going over there, because I might say something that would be bad for the insurance.

I tapped Joaquin on the shoulder. "Did you like the book?" It was his left hand that was scarred, as opposed to Johnny Tremain's right. My scar only showed in a bathing suit, which in fifth grade was no big deal. Later, my mother said, it would be, and I'd want plastic surgery. That was what the money we got was for.

Joaquin turned around to face me. His eyes were black

and opaque like a pony's. But I could see he knew which book I meant, though in Gifted and Talented we read a ton. "I don't want to talk about it," he said, which is what Johnny Tremain says to Cilla before he marches off to fight the British.

"You saved Joaquin's life," Julia says, when I finish telling her the story. We're lying on the bed in my room. "Maybe it's a family tradition, and you guys will get married."

Talking about marriage at our age is like discussing whether you'd want to be in an open coffin or cremated. But I laugh, to cover up the fact that I'm turning red. "I don't think Sam would like that," I say.

Mrs. Marshall, my babysitter, is downstairs. You might think that a nearly sixteen-year-old girl who is sexually active wouldn't need a babysitter, but my mother says that's exactly who needs one.

Julia sits up. "Is Sam the jealous type?" Her eyes are glittery from her medication. On the days she forgets to take it she buzzes around the room like a trapped fly.

"Not so much," I say. "We are in love, though." Sam is a senior, and his parents worried that the intensity of our relationship would affect his grades during this crucial fall semester. So they drew up a contract stating that he would hang out with me two school afternoons a week. The other three he would go to the library. That has become our code for sex: going to the library.

"Can I see your scar?" Julia asks me.

I sit up too and start to take off my shirt and bra.

"What about that old lady?" Julia glances nervously at my open bedroom door.

"Mrs. Marshall? She has arthritis and can't climb the stairs."

Mrs. Marshall is also pretty deaf, plus you could walk by her with a bong the size of a tuba and she wouldn't notice. I kind of love her. I think I was an old lady in a previous life. It would be easy for me to sneak Sam up to my room, but I don't want to get her fired. Her grandson has PTSD, but the money hasn't come through yet.

"It's like it's our patriotic duty not to go up there," I said once to Sam. He's thinking of going into the military instead of college, despite his great GPA. His parents would die if they knew.

"Your problem is that you're too nice, Edith," Sam said. "To everyone but me," he added pitifully.

"What do you say we go to the library in your car?"

"I'd say you was the sweetest gal in the world and ah loves you to pieces," Sam said, in a half-hillbilly, half-African-American accent. But I still think that counts as saying the word.

My philosophy is why not do what people want and make them happy if it doesn't hurt anything and you have the time? My mother would be stunned to hear this, though, because according to her, I'm stubborn as a mule. I still won't agree to the plastic surgery, for example.

Maybe the truth about me is that I have no idea what I'll do until after I've done it.

Now I'm sitting on the bed with my top off while Julia gazes at my chest with her big, dark eyes. "Does Sam mind it?" she asks.

"No," I say. "He says it's like a 3-D tattoo, and that I should get cobra fangs inked on the end." My scar is a ropy ridge of skin that snakes around under one breast.

"I can see how that would look really good," Julia says, nodding. "But maybe you should wait. Another guy might not like it."

Just then we hear my dad's car pull into the driveway, and I scramble to put my shirt back on. "I am so glad you're a girl," I say, as we clatter down the back stairs.

"If I was Joaquin, whole 'nother story," Julia says.

When I hear that I almost fall down the stairs. But there isn't time to ask what she means. My dad's in the kitchen, pouring out a splash of Booker's. He'll have a proper one later, with my mother, after driving the babysitter home.

"Any trouble with Naughty Edith?" he asks Mrs. Marshall, as he hugs me. This is their nightly comedy routine.

"She was pretty good today," Mrs. Marshall says. "I only had to beat her once." Then she and my dad laugh, and Mrs. Marshall slips her book into her canvas tote. It isn't exactly pornography that she reads, but I was shocked when I picked it up once while she was in the bathroom.

"I'm going to the library afterward," my dad says to me. "You girls want to come?"

Well, Julia and I go into complete hysterics. "Oh, Mr. Newman," she chokes out finally. "It would not be at all appropriate for us to come with you to the library."

"You two sure enjoy life," he says, smiling uncertainly. I can see he's a little hurt to be left out of the joke, but only a little. It's my mother who zeroes in on the smallest raised eyebrow, demanding to be told. She's another force of nature.

My dad holds the car door for Mrs. Marshall. "Thank you, kind sir," she says, like one of the historically inaccurate damsels in her books. Soon enough she'll be home and in for another rough night with her grandson. Old as she is, she cried when she told me about him.

It's barely five o'clock but already dark as Julia and I shuffle through the dead leaves to the Roths'. The four of us hang out there every day now that Chipotle has become infested with ninth-graders. "Where are their parents?" we'd say loudly, and they'd give us stupid, childish stares. But we can't go to Sam's, or my place, and even I have never been inside Julia's house. All she'll say is that she's the least heavily medicated person in her family, including the dog.

"Just don't even ask," she says, so I haven't. On the other hand, I've told her everything she wanted to know about Sam and me. My dad says this aspect of my personality will save me from a life of crime: If you ask me a question, I'll answer it. I'll give examples and show all my work.

We're two blocks from Joaquin's when I finally come out with it: "What you were saying on the stairs—"

Julia turns to me, smiling beautifully. Under the street-lamp, her breath makes a cloud around her head. "Oh, about Joaquin," she says. "You should know this before you marry him, Edith: All he wants to do is look. It's kind of weird." She touches my arm. "I'm freezing—let's run."

While Julia and I are running, I'll backtrack: One spring afternoon in eighth grade, Joaquin knocked on our front door. At that time, I didn't have a babysitter.

He didn't need to tell me his mother had breast cancer. All the women in the neighborhood had rallied—making casseroles, driving him to the orthodontist. I wouldn't say my mother was glad Joaquin's mother was sick, but she was grateful there was an opportunity to pitch in and prove she wasn't a horrible person. Most people had sided with the Roths in the lawsuit.

Joaquin held up a pack of cards. "Do you want to play Yu-Gi-Oh!?" he asked, a little sheepishly.

I understood—it's like watching reruns of Blue's Clues when you're home with a cold. So he came in, and we sat down at our dining room table, and before long I'd won almost the whole deck. The game is pure luck, though when we were little it had seemed full of strategy and magic. We used to talk about it for hours.

"This is dumb," Joaquin said. He glanced around our dining room. "Everything's the same here."

"Yes. Except the walls are a different color and we have a new table and chairs."

He made a face like that was the most nitpicky thing he'd ever heard. "Do you know how to play strip poker?"

"Not really."

"Well, it's easy."

That was how it started. Every day Joaquin came over and we played. We didn't touch, and we mostly only spoke about poker. I had some idea that this was helping him cope, seeing me naked with my healed scar, but I don't really know. When boys hit puberty, they stop talking. But that was how I tried to explain it to my mother.

She'd come home from work early to make lentils for the Roths, and we never heard her walk in.

"Joaquin, you need to go home now," she said, very calmly. The funny thing was that he didn't seem flustered, but then he did still have his boxers on. He pulled on his jeans and T-shirt, gave me a hang-in-there smile, and left.

"You and I need to talk, young lady." She was still so calm, I was terrified. My hands shook as I put on my clothes. "Do you need birth control pills, Edith?" she asked.

"No! Mom, I swear!"

"If and when you do, will you tell me?" She didn't wait for an answer. She stood and went into the kitchen.

That was it. I was free to go. But she hired Mrs. Marshall, about whom I threw a massive tantrum before I met her. "I'm sorry, sweetie," my mother said. "It's tough love."

Her calmness was just a phase, though. Last summer, after I had hooked up with Sam, and she was driving me to get the prescription, she kept saying over and over in a shaky voice,

"I'm at my wits' end. What would you do, if you had a daughter?"

I couldn't help her. I felt bad, the way a judge probably feels bad sending a murderer to the electric chair, but the law is the law. The law of teenagers is that they won't not do something simply because their parents don't want them to. There's got to be another reason.

Julia and I burst into the Roths' kitchen, red from the cold and panting. "Like a pair of Dianas," Mrs. Roth says—the kind of random comment that makes Julia crazy. She's reading a cooking magazine, but there are no ingredients out, nothing on the stove. Her hair has grown back now and she wears it long, and a lot of floaty clothes that can't be described by words like shirt, pants, or skirt. "The great lesson of cancer is that you stop caring what people think," she told us once, and of course Julia had to mutter to me, "I'd care if I was her."

"The boys are in the basement," Mrs. Roth says. "Let the wild rumpus start."

I recognize the quote from Joaquin's old favorite book and laugh politely, but something isn't right with her expression, as if behind the cooking magazine she's reading something tragic.

I turn away quickly and follow Julia down the basement steps.

Sam and Joaquin are watching several TiVo'd shows at

once, something that makes me carsick, and I hop onto Sam's lap. "I like a woman you can really get ahold of," he says. He's always complimentary of my build, but does he have to mention it every single time?

It's late October and the four of us have been hanging out since Labor Day, but it feels like decades, like this could segue into shuffleboard at the Home. It's so simple and comfortable. We don't sit in tight, exclusive pairs like middle-schoolers but cuddle and sprawl all over each other like Sam's college-age siblings do with their friends.

That partly explains why I don't notice—until I think about it later—how wildly Sam and Julia are flirting, exchanging little pats, adding little jokes to the conversation that only they laugh at. Meanwhile, I'm on autopilot, chewing over what Julia told me. Do she and Joaquin play cards, or what? Listening to the four of us goofing around, you'd never guess that one couple is having sex and the other isn't. Because sex is the subtext to everything we say, and in that regard Joaquin seems completely normal. Or am I the easy lay who isn't? I feel the baffled alarm of the dream where you're in class with no clothes on—why did nobody tell me everyone else would be dressed?

I sort of wake up when I realize there's panic in the room—Julia says it's her turn to make dinner tonight, and she totally forgot. "They're going to kill me," she whimpers. I have no idea who "they" are, but I picture a whole crazy family coming at her with steak knives.

"I'll drive you," Sam says to Julia. "I could drop you on the way," he says to me, but with a look that suggests that delaying could be a matter of life and death.

"No worries," I say. "I'll walk home."

Away they go.

Joaquin and I are still sitting at opposite ends of the old corduroy sofa, which is living out its retirement years in the basement. The purple Magic Marker stains were made by me.

"Talk about your transparent maneuvers," Joaquin says.

"I didn't know Julia could cook."

"She can't," he says.

I'm no faster on the uptake than I was at age nine, but finally, finally, I understand what's happened literally under my nose. I don't cry, though. I must be in shock. My hands are clammy and my breathing feels shallow.

"Why the fake drama?" I say. "Why not just announce that they're through with us and want to go out with each other?"

"She's your friend," Joaquin says. "Ex-friend, I guess." He gets up and stretches, as if all this had actually been a bizarre dream. "I'd better start my homework."

"Fuck them both," I say. "And I mean that in the nicest possible way."

Joaquin is partway up the basement steps, and he stops and looks at me. "You're funny, Edith," he says. Then he turns and keeps on going.

* * *

After a while I turn off the basement lights and come upstairs, where Mr. Roth is stirring a pot on the stove. "Helen wasn't feeling well, and she went to lie down," Mr. Roth says, as if his presence in the kitchen needs explanation. Helen? Oh, Mrs. Roth. "So I am melting the frozen soup your mother kindly prepared."

"She was happy to do it." Which is, I think, exactly what my mother would have wanted me to say.

Mr. Roth has a big, sad, craggy face that seems to belong on a monument. "I can empathize with your mother," he says. "I, too, was a member of the political opposition."

Sometimes Mr. Roth is hard to understand, even though his English is fluent, but at last I realize what he's driving at. "Mom feels like she's the only Republican in Maryland," I say. "She used to put out yard signs to annoy my dad, but now she says politics has gotten too brutal."

He smiles a little. "It could be worse," he says. Joaquin once told me that a friend of his dad's who was a leftist in Argentina was pushed by soldiers from a plane into the ocean.

"May I have a glass of water?" I say.

"Allow me." He pours a glass from a pitcher in the fridge and puts a little saucer under it. When he sets it on the counter I can see the marks on his wrists where he was tortured, though Mr. Roth doesn't know I know about this. Despite all the childhood hours I spent here, we haven't had many conversations.

All four people in this house are ruined specimens, I think suddenly. I might be the most ruined of all—in some cultures, my father would have to kill me if he knew I wasn't a virgin. As it is, my mother hasn't told him because she says it would break his heart.

Well, my heart is broken.

"Julia and Sam ditched Joaquin and me and are probably cheating on us this very second," I burst out. I feel I can say this because Mr. Roth probably has no idea what I'm talking about or even who Julia and Sam are.

"Julia is a very self-centered girl, and Sam is a very conventional boy," he says. "Whereas Joaquin, and you—" he trails off. I've often been told that this is my effect on people: I leave them speechless. But I'm speechless now too, with astonishment.

"I should check on Helen," Mr. Roth says, after a moment. "Is it all right to leave the pot unattended?" This is my cue to go on home.

"If you set the flame very low and put a lid on, it should be fine."

"Thank you, Edith," he says. He walks me to the front door. "What I meant to say is, I'm convinced you and Joaquin will accomplish great things when you grow up."

That's what parents always say, isn't it? Because it's pretty much life and death with them—that all their attention and worry turn out to be worth it. "At least I'll be a great defroster of soup," I say.

As I head down the brick walk I can see Joaquin sitting at

his father's desk in his second-floor study. I wonder if he'll grow up to be a writer too—if he's also observing everyone secretly and someday will explain it, this big mess between Sam and Julia and him and me. I'd read that book.

Or maybe his dad's study is where the graphing calculator is.

I'm standing under the streetlamp when he looks up and sees me. He raises his left hand—which is stiff and strange-looking even at this distance—and waves. He could mean, See you tomorrow in precalculus. He could mean, Have a nice life. He could mean, Someday, Edith, I'll love you back.

Milagros

After his last book came out George called me to say that he'd had it—with the ringing phone, the idiotic interview questions, the ghastly parties—would I please run away to Mexico with him? He'd heard about an undiscovered hotel on an island in the Caribbean. "I know you like to swim, Mila, and of course you speak the language," he said. "So I've reserved two rooms with sea views."

I saw all the years, as a drowning person is said to, in which I'd been in love with George. There'd been a time when I was so enamored that I'd lie on his bed and watch him type. Sometimes he'd look up and then come over and make love to me, like someone who's just remembered to walk the dog or move the car to the other side of the street. Lately, we'd agreed to be friends, but I was surprised that he'd invited me to Mexico. Usually he had more than one love affair going, which was the same way he wrote his novels.

Anyway, I agreed to go. I'd just finished translating a ponderous Chilean novel, and I thought it might be good to get out of my apartment. Manhattan is an island of hermits. Accompanying George would be like a translating job, except I could have fun with it. I imagined interpreting for him if he tried to pick up a beautiful woman in a seaside bar. *¿Cuál es tu signo astrológico?* I'd tell her he wanted to know and then turn to him with a puzzled shrug as she walked away.

I met George when I came to New York after college twelve years ago, and like everyone else I knew there, he was working a shit job and writing a novel. Because he was forty, his ambition seemed poignant, like a middle-aged man thinking he could be a rock star. But he made me laugh, and since I wasn't writing a novel myself, his preposterous hopes didn't depress me too much.

In those days we spent a lot of time in Cuban diners, talking about his characters. I helped him invent backstories for his women. I told him what kind of underwear a Cuban secretary in her fifties might have, how a Latina teenager would apply makeup. Our women were complicated and interesting—more so, I felt, than the ones who ended up on his pages.

"The thing is, Mila, editors are ruthless jackals." This opinion of his never changed.

"But does Maria have to die horribly in chapter three?"

"I'm afraid so. Can you think of one novel where the protagonist just happily lives her life, and nothing goes wrong?"

I couldn't, but it had always seemed to me that I would enjoy reading a book like that.

Then the unbelievable thing happened: George sold his book for a lot of money. Everything changed, and nothing did. Over lunch at The Pierre, he still complained; now it was about how fame was a burden, how he didn't know who his real friends were, how everyone wanted a piece of him. I told him the least I could do was relieve him of the burden of having sex with me.

George put down his fork and turned red. I'd said this as a joke, to shut him up, but I'd hit a nerve I didn't know was there. The evening ended awkwardly, and we didn't speak for a long time afterward. At last, he called. "I miss you, Mila. Couldn't we be friends?"

If we were to be friends, I said, we would have to talk about me sometimes.

"Absolutely," George said. "What aspect of yourself would you like to talk about?"

"Well, I'm taking swimming lessons."

"You can't swim?" George said. "I didn't know that."

At college we were supposed to be able to swim twenty-five yards in order to graduate—a stipulation of a benefactor whose son had gone down on the Titanic—but I had gotten a dispensation. "Now I can swim a length without stopping," I told George. "I really like it." I liked that predictable back and forth, back and forth, like a goldfish.

"Congratulations, Mila," George said. He sounded genuinely pleased for me, and I realized I'd missed him too. Then we talked about the unfairness of ebook contracts until his agent called on the other line, and he had to go.

George and I had arranged to meet at the departure gate at Kennedy, and he came running up after all the other passengers had boarded. He's tall and thin, and if you line up his book-jacket photos next to each other, the only change is his fair hairline, receding gradually up his forehead like a waning tide. He gazed at me confusedly, and then we kissed on both cheeks, though neither of us has lived in Europe.

"You look fantastic, Mila," he said. But he still looked confused, a little alarmed.

"Thanks—I feel great too." I smoothed the skirt of my new size-four sundress.

"Thank God," he said. Then he smiled. "For a minute there I was afraid you had cancer and I'd have to carry your luggage the whole trip."

"Would you folks mind continuing your joyful reunion in your seats?" the gate agent said.

"Not at all," George said. "Hurry it up there, Mila."

So my losing fifty pounds wasn't going to change things between us—any more than his money and celebrity had. That was reassuring, I told myself, as I hoisted my bag into the overhead bin.

On the plane, I described to George how I'd dropped the weight by swimming a mile a day. He took out his Moleskine and made some notes. I guessed his next book would have a female character who went from fat to fabulous—before she turned up dismembered in a dumpster.

"You didn't follow any diets?" George said.

I shook my head. "Actually, I'm less hungry than I used to be."

"You should go on Oprah."

"Don't tease."

"I'm serious. Next time I see her I'll mention you."

From the hot, chaotic Mexican airport we rode a bus that rattled south along the eastern coast. George read aloud from a guidebook while I looked out the window. Flashes of turquoise water glinted behind copses of ragged banana palms. On the other side of all that water was Cuba, my native country. Ruled by the Devil Incarnate, according to my Aunt Isabel, who had raised me in Miami after my parents died. How pleased she would have been to know that the Devil was now a weak, raspy-voiced old man. Isabel had died in her robust prime, of a stroke.

"There's the ruin I was just reading about," George was saying. He tapped my shoulder. "Are you asleep?"

"I was thinking about my Aunt Isabel," I said. "The one who became Aunt Carmen in your novel."

"I love Aunt Carmen," George said. In his book, she becomes the victim of a diabolical serial killer.

After my aunt died, I'd regretted that she was immortalized by what I'd revealed about her to George—the girdle and pointy bras, the right-wing politics, the obsessive good manners. Although now there was talk of J.Lo playing her in the movie.

Late in the afternoon the bus pulled up to the ferry landing, where a boat would take us to the island. The smell of grilled meat wafted toward us from food carts at the end of the dock. "I'm going to get a taco," I said. "Do you want one?"

George shook his head. "I'm going to try and avoid Mexican food."

"Isn't all the food in Mexico Mexican?"

"Not at the hotel, surely," George said. "It costs the earth."

Most of our fellow passengers didn't look like they were headed to a resort. Small and weather-beaten, they were carrying baskets and bundles and even chickens in wire cages. Perhaps the place really was undiscovered. Then I noticed a chubby girl of about seven and her toddler brother jumping from bench to bench on the deck of the ferry. They were blond, and their summer outfits looked expensive and new. A handsome man in a polo shirt pleaded in Spanish for them to sit down.

"We're not hurting anything," the girl retorted in English.

"But you might fall into the water! Come, *aquí son los* Game Boys."

"Game Boys?" George muttered. "For a ten-minute ride?"

"Cubans don't believe it's bad to spoil children," I said. "They think you ought to have happy memories you can fall back on." Despite being an orphan, I had nothing but happy memories—I was pampered and cosseted by Aunt Isabel and the flock of pink-collar Cubanas who were her friends.

The Cuban father glanced across the deck at George and me. *Gente como uno,* his look said—people like us.

"You can tell the guy's Cuban because of his accent," George declared authoritatively. He hated not knowing things.

I nodded and the man smiled, though he couldn't have heard us. "Widowed or amicably divorced," I said. "Otherwise his ex-wife wouldn't have let him travel with the kids."

"Maybe you should be a writer, Mila, instead of a translator."

"I can't make things up."

"Who says I make things up?" George said.

My hotel room was three times the size of my apartment. Slatted French doors led to a balcony overlooking the ocean, which hissed and slapped at the sand. My bed was vast as Texas and sexily curtained with mosquito netting. I lay down and suddenly felt the waste of it, as if I were sending half a filet mignon back to the kitchen at The Pierre. Why had George brought me, instead of a twenty-something starlet who'd played one of his prematurely deceased characters?

The phone beside the bed rang. "Do you like your room?"

"It's perfect."

"Well, mine isn't. My view isn't really of the ocean. You can see a little wedge of it, but mostly it's of the pool."

"I'll change with you, if you want."

"No, I've already used the bathroom." It was odd how once you stopped being lovers with someone their most private quirks receded from memory. "I'll give the front desk a piece of my mind in the morning," George said, meaning that I would. Here was one thing I could do that a starlet couldn't: give a Mexican desk clerk a piece of George's mind.

Suddenly, I heard his phone clatter to the tiled floor and footsteps. Then a choking, gagging sound. My heart flailed. What a terrible irony if George were meeting a fate like one he had written. Then I heard water running, and he came back on the line. "Mila, I am so sick," he whispered hoarsely.

"I'll be right there."

He was very pale, laid out on his bed as if on a bier. I opened his fridge, and he flinched a little. George could be generous, but he had a streak of cheapness: he hated paying minibar prices. Nevertheless, I removed a Coke and poured some into a glass.

"Take small sips," I said. "It's probably a twenty-four-hour stomach bug."

"But I've eaten no Mexican food! You breathed on me with your taco breath, though. Did you know that when you smell something, the molecules are actually *inside* your nose? If you smell dog crap, it means—"

"You'll feel better if you sleep," I said. When I handed him the Coke, his fingers felt like live coals, but I didn't say so. I set the glass back on the nightstand and tucked the mosquito netting in around the mattress. Through the gauze he looked as he had when I first met him, a rakish blond editor of scripts for industrial videos. I was the translator for the Spanish versions. There'd be at least one woman on every project who'd fall for him, and they'd date for a while until he found something wrong with her.

"Typhoid fever," the hotel doctor pronounced the next morning.

"How long do I have?" George asked, his face ivory against the white pillows. He looked resigned and holy.

"A week," the doctor said. "Less, if you take the Cipro according to instructions." He glanced from George to me and chuckled. "Why do Americans always think typhoid is a death sentence?"

"Blame Paul Bowles," George said. "Writers ought to be more responsible about killing their characters."

The doctor turned to me. "Typhoid is a salmonella-bacterium infection. Very treatable. Make sure he gets plenty of fluids."

"I knew it was the fumes from that taco yesterday," George said, giving me a look that was at once accusatory and forgiving.

"The incubation period is fourteen days, so you must have caught it in America," the doctor said cheerfully. Our gringo ignorance had made his day.

I read aloud two *Vanity Fair* articles about people George knew, and fetched ruinously priced soft drinks from the fridge. I asked if he wanted me to go complain about his room. "I can't be moved," he moaned, with his eyes closed. I began an article about the banking crisis, and halfway through he asked me to call room service for broth.

When it came, I said, "I'm not going to feed you unless you open your eyes."

George stared as though he hadn't realized who I was. "What are you doing inside on such a beautiful day, Mila? I'm ordering you to the beach."

"I don't mind staying in," I said, truthfully, but I went back to my room and put on my bathing suit, the faded one-piece I swam laps in. It would look silly on the beach, I realized. Growing up in Miami, I never went to the beach. Aunt Isabel wasn't a beach person, and she was quite sure I wasn't.

"*Imagínense,* after what she's been through," she'd say softly to the other aunties sitting on her shaded patio in their linen summer shifts and pearls.

"Imagine, poor little Milagros," they murmured, casting liquid-brown gazes at orphaned me, curled in the glider with *The Long Winter.* Overcome with tenderness and pity, one of them would fix me a glass of lemonade and a second slice of *tres leches* cake.

I took a bottle of water from my fridge and put the hotel's terry robe on over my suit and walked out along the breeze-way to the edge of the sand. The two Cuban children from the ferry darted past me, and behind them trudged their father, bearing two inflated rings with sea-monster heads and wearing an expression of determined patience. "Careful!" he called, just as his daughter tripped, went sprawling, then wailed with sand in her mouth. I hurried toward her with my water bottle.

"You're all right," I said in Spanish, the language of consolation. "Rinse and spit."

In an instant the Cuban man was kneeling beside me. "Which is the saint who carries water?" he said.

"Saint Evian, I think."

"I'm Mario," he said. "Give the auntie a thank-you kiss, Blanca."

Blanca put her sweaty arms around my neck. Cuban kids might be spoiled, but we're trained to kiss on command.

"My name is Milagros—Mila," I said.

"We've met before," Mario said.

"On the ferry."

He shook his head. "Before that. You must be from Miami. What school did you go to?"

"Sacred Heart," I said. "I did my First Communion at Saint Eulalia's." As I rattled off possible Cuban-exile connections, something lurched inside me like a falling elevator. My only contact with that world now were the glitter-encrusted birthday cards I still got from the aunties. "Did you take dancing classes with Señorita Alarcón?"

"Señorita Alarcón!" Mario exclaimed. He had a gorgeous smile. "The box step and the cha-cha. Warm Hawaiian Punch. You were a skinny girl with braids?"

"A fat girl with curls."

"A beauty, surely! Anyway, I'm a bit older than you. But we have met, somewhere."

"Daddy!" the little boy called. "Beach!" He looked hot and desperate, but I didn't know Mario well enough to ask if he'd remembered the sunscreen.

"*Momentito*, my love."

"Go ahead," I said. "I'm going to swim in the pool."

"We want to go to the pool with the auntie!" Blanca cried.

"No, my darling. We're going to swim in the lovely sea."

"I hate the lovely sea!"

They'll be at the pool in five minutes, I thought.

They were. Blanca proposed to Mario junior that they chase me in their sea-monster rings as I swam laps. After three lengths of this, I got out and sat in a chaise beside Mario.

"You're quite a swimmer," Mario said. "And I can see you're good with children." I'd been told this before, but it's really that children, like cats, can sense when someone doesn't care for them and they go straight for that person.

"And their mother?" I asked.

"Not in the picture," Mario said softly. He turned his brilliant smile on me again. "Is the gentleman you were with on the ferry your husband?" he said.

"An old friend," I said. "I came along to translate for him. He writes thrillers. He's sick at the moment." The more I said, the odder my relationship with George sounded.

"Ah," Mario said. "Well, it would be nice if you both could

join us for dinner. Or if he's still under the weather, just you."

* * *

Blanca and Mario junior choked down the required minimum of one bite of the lobster platters they had insisted upon, and left the table. Using their silverware, Blanca directed her brother in a pharaonic digging project on the sand floor of the hotel restaurant.

Mario and I sat across from each other in the flickering candlelight. We exchanged tidily edited versions of our life stories. He poured me a second glass of wine. We laughed. Palm trees rustled softly overhead.

It might have looked and sounded as though we were on a date. George was certain that we were.

"Don't be ridiculous," I'd said, after telling him about Mario's invitation. "He asked specifically for you to come too. I'm going to sign for my own meal." Then I realized this meant that George would be paying for it. He realized it too.

"I'm glad to pay—all I want is for you to be happy, Mila."

I put my hand on his forehead. His fever seemed a bit lower. "I'll be back to check on you in an hour," I said.

"It was a mistake to come here," George said plaintively.

"It's only a few more days," I said.

"But how horrible, to be counting the days until your vacation is over!"

"Well, I'm having a nice time," I said.

George grunted and turned toward the wall, his desire for my happiness already evaporated.

* * *

I began to feel like Eloise, like I'd always lived at an expensive hotel. This was my new life: reading to George until noon; a swim in the pool; lunch with Mario and the children; reading to George in the afternoon; another swim; dinner with Mario and the children. I finished all the reading material George had brought and started him on *The Small House at Allington.*

"Nothing's happening," he grumbled. "How can you like this stuff?"

Actually, I liked Trollope best before the love affairs and misunderstandings began—when it was just the women sitting around in their morning dresses, writing letters and planning luncheon. Of course, real Victorian life wasn't so idyllic—even aristocrats smelled bad and never washed their hair, and if they got typhoid, they died.

Between Mario and me, it was a somewhat Victorian courtship, continually chaperoned by Blanca and Mario junior. Still, I warmed to them. Blanca sat in my lap and arranged my hair, announcing she'd wear hers just like this when she was old. Mario junior brought me a pebble he'd found, then stood a little way off, grinning furiously as I praised it.

Suddenly his face crumpled. "*¡Mamá!*"

Blanca jumped down and ran to him. "*No está, tonto.*"

"Where is she?" I mouthed to Mario.

"Houston, I believe," he said, and sighed. "It's always changing."

"That's rough on you," I said. The children clambered onto his knees, and he kissed their sandy heads.

"Sometimes." But plainly, he adored them.

Mostly, Mario and I talked about Cuba—a place I didn't remember and he'd never been. But his family, like mine, had owned an estate in the *campo*, and he'd seen the photographs, so it was as if he had ridden horseback through fields of sugarcane and been awakened every morning by a maid bringing coffee on a Spanish silver tray.

"That's what Aunt Isabel always remembered," I said. "Breakfast in bed, like in a hotel."

"As soon as the bastard's gone, we'll go back," Mario said, including me and the children with a sweep of his Roman-profile head. "Before my father died, he drew a map of where in the garden the silver was buried."

All through my childhood I'd heard this kind of talk: We'll go back and reclaim it—air out the linen cupboard and polish the floors and prune the jasmine, and all will be as it was. As a teenager, I'd argued with Aunt Isabel: It's gone and we'll never get it back. It's better that the Cuban people own it.

I made her cry, saying that. And who was Isabel hurting, really, driving along Biscayne Boulevard in her orange Datsun, harboring fantasies of a vanished world? She was the most kindhearted person I'd ever known. So I didn't argue with Mario. I sat on the chaise by the pool, with the tropical breezes brushing my skin, and let his inherited nostalgia wash right over me.

* * *

I was dressing for dinner when Mario knocked on the door of my room. Tomorrow we were all leaving the island. But it wouldn't be good-bye, Mario said, and he'd kept adding brushstrokes to his picture of a future in which I was chatelaine and stepmother on a reclaimed Cuban sugar plantation.

"Where are the children?" I'd put on my perfume last, as Aunt Isabel had taught me, to make an impression.

"Playing with their Game Boys in the room." He looked at me anxiously. "Don't you think they'd be all right for a few minutes?"

I wasn't their stepmother yet. "You're the one raising them."

"Yes." He cocked his head, smiled, and I stood aside and let him in. "I've realized who you are," he said.

"Rumpelstiltskin," I said.

"No—" For a moment he wore the same baffled expression Mario junior did when his sister sneaked up behind and shoved him. "You are Baby Milagros. I used to see you on TV."

"You're right," I said.

He put his arms around me and we swayed, as if Señorita Alarcón were about to drop the needle on the foxtrot: *Uno, dos, tres.*

"You were the first girl I was in love with," Mario said.

Well—maybe I was. I thought of plump, bossy Blanca, whose worshipful brother would have dug sand all night with a teaspoon.

I shrugged and smiled, and we made our way to my big bed.

I don't remember the most dramatic event of my life, but you might: the news stories thirty years ago about Baby Milagros, found floating in an inner tube by a fisherman off the Florida coast. In the Miami exile community, I became a symbol of freedom, a miracle who had escaped the Devil. Every year, on the anniversary of my rescue, I was interviewed for Spanish-language newspapers and television programs, affirming that, although I'd survived sixteen hours alone in the sea, I still didn't know how to swim. *Un milagro.*

"I ought to have known you immediately, Milagros," Mario said. He touched my face with the side of his finger. "Your cheeks still have baby fat."

"Mario—the children!" I sat up. "It's been much more than a few minutes."

He got up and began putting on his clothes, but unhurriedly. "It's all right. They're with their mother."

"I don't understand. You sent them to Houston?"

"That leg of Melody's sales trip got cancelled, actually. She came directly here from Omaha." He wasn't looking at me, but at the crisp cuffs of his shirt as he folded them back over his wrists. "But you know, I think it will be fine. Since George is feeling better, I made reservations for all of us to have dinner tonight. It turns out Melody is a huge fan of George Paddock's novels."

I couldn't take in what he was saying. "You're not divorced," I said stupidly. "Your wife was traveling for business."

"We were supposed to meet up tomorrow night in Cancún, but Melody decided to surprise us," Mario said. A fissure of chagrin appeared on his glossy surface. "I admit it was a surprise." He pressed his lips together.

"And you're not really planning to go back to Cuba."

"Do you think I was just saying that, to seduce you? Not true! Melody and I have our issues. She's Anglo, and she says wouldn't move to Cuba if Jesus himself became the next president. So who knows what the future holds?"

"For you, *la putamadre que te parió.*"

He took a step back toward the bed. "Don't be angry, Mila. I thought we were on the same page. You come here with one man, and the minute he gets sick you go off with another."

"That's different. George knows about you. He encouraged me to spend time with you!"

"You know, the whole open-relationship scene is just too bizarre for me," Mario said. "Call me old-fashioned." He was standing by the door, surveying me from his moral high ground as I lay there brazenly with nothing on. "In fact, I think we should cancel dinner."

I pulled the sheet up over my head and lay still. After a long silence, I heard the door click shut. The palm fronds began to clatter in a rising wind. When I looked out, clouds were scuttling across a red evening sky.

Shortly after ten, George called. Our routine, in our typhoid-at-the-resort life, was that I'd look in on him after dinner, plump his pillows and make sure he'd taken his evening Cipro. "You don't sound good," he said.

"Mario came by, and I lost track of the time."

"Ah." A low chuckle. Then, tentatively, "Are you alone now?"

"Yes."

"Well, I won't ruin the afterglow. I just want to say that you two make a very attractive couple, sitting by the pool. And it's amazing the way you rattle away in Spanish."

What amazed me was the idea of George rising from his sickbed to watch us from his window. "That's why you invited me to Mexico, isn't it?" I said. "So I could use my Spanish?"

"That was kind of why," George said, and sighed.

I'd always told myself that at the right moment I'd tell George about Baby Milagros. But those moments kept passing, and suddenly his books were everywhere. I didn't mourn or miss my family, yet I couldn't bear the thought that the tale of their drowning might end up for sale on the sidewalk outside Zabar's, or in paperback at Duane Reade, next to the cough drops.

The wind blew hard all night, banging the shutters on the French doors. As soon as it was light, I went down to George's room and tapped on the door.

"Come in!" he called. It was his regular, healthy voice. Next to the bed was a laden room-service cart: a platter of *huevos rancheros* with *chorizo*, orange juice, papaya halves with lime, tortillas, *pan dulce*, toast, ham, a pot of *café con leche*. "I woke up with this appetite," he said. "We could order something for you too." He hesitated. "I thought you'd be having breakfast with Mario."

"No," I said. "I've got a story for you, though." I poured myself a cup of coffee and sat down in my reading chair beside the bed. While George ate, I explained about how Cuban former plantation owners sent their sons and daughters to the same schools and dancing classes in Miami. The idea was that we'd meet and marry each other and pass along property maps and memories of buried silver trays. But neither Mario nor I had done what we were supposed to. I'd escaped to New York, and he'd married an Anglo wife who worked and traveled and had the nerve to show up unexpectedly and spoil his love affairs.

I poured a second cup of coffee and surveyed the ruins of the breakfast cart. While I'd been talking—ranting, really—George had devoured every morsel. "You didn't want anything to eat, did you?" he said.

"No. But thanks for the thought."

He was eating guava jam straight from the jar with a spoon. "It's my fault, Mila," he said at last.

"I'm thirty-two years old, George. If I want a piece of toast, I'll ask."

"I was talking about Mario." He set down the jam jar, and his robe parted to reveal chest hair that was entirely white. When had that happened? "In your twenties, when you should have been learning about cads, you were with me."

Once, years ago, after we'd had a few drinks, I'd asked

George if he'd ever been interested in men. Given how touchy he could be, I was surprised that he didn't take offense. "People wonder that, if you're good-looking enough," he'd said musingly. "But this much I do know: Definitely not."

George wanted to be able to say he'd at least set foot on the sand, so before the last ferry sailed, we went to the beach. It was overcast and the wind was cold, and the beach was deserted. Mario and his family sensibly must have left for the mainland before whatever hurricane was brewing hit. If the children asked about me, he would say to his wife, "George Paddock's assistant. She was great with the kids." But they'd probably already forgotten me.

"Isn't this pleasant," George said, as stinging sand hit our faces. "You know, if you lie flat, you can feel a tiny bit of warmth."

I laughed then, and enshrouded myself with a towel. George lay on his back, his thin, pale legs sticking out of baggy trunks. "You might think I've been lounging around all week," he said. "But writers are working even when they're staring out the window."

"I've heard that before, somewhere."

He waved his hand as if at a gnat, and began talking about his next book, which would be set at an elegant resort in Mexico. At the end of the first chapter, just as the reader is getting to know and like them, a family of four from Miami would be savagely murdered.

"Oh, George, not the children!" I cried.

"It's a novel," George said. "Since when do you care about children, anyway?"

"Didn't I ever tell you how my parents and my little brother and I left Cuba?"

"No." He raised himself up on one elbow. "And you've never said you had a brother."

"I thought I had." I wasn't looking at him. Far out on the water, Blanca and Mario junior's abandoned sea monsters bobbed among the whitecaps. *This is not a lifesaving device* was printed on the rings in various languages, but that wasn't true. Here I was.

"Name one thing you've told me that I've forgotten, ever," George said. He touched my knee, and his eyes, when I met his gaze, were almost beseeching.

I shook my head. "I can't." This was what George could offer me: the fact that he listened. Plus his jokes and his wealth, of course. Now I realized he'd brought me to Mexico with some idea of laying it all at my feet. Before Mario, it might have seemed enough.

So a cad is good for something: a taste of what you might have if you fell in love for real. But if I did fall in love, George would have to be part of the package, like a crazy *abuela* from the old country, living in a room off the kitchen.

It was a sentimental notion; very Cuban and very impractical. In my imagined future, I missed George already, and tears started in my eyes.

"Don't fuss, Mila, for God's sake," he said, and withdrew his hand. "Forget I said anything. And if it means that much to you, I'll spare the children."

Homebody

When my sister, Leticia, and I were little, our father, Pepe, adored us, but it was our mother, Rosa, whom we craved. Mama was child-sized herself, with abundant, shiny dark hair. Sharp-faced and sharp-tongued, she couldn't bear us on her lap for more than a minute before exclaiming, "Ay, *chicas,* your bones are clacking on my bones!" (Years later, after Leticia's remains were dug from a mass grave on the outskirts of Buenos Aires, that was the phrase that kept whipping like a cold pampas wind through my head).

Usually Mama avoided being touched, but when there were no customers in the grocery store, we'd press close on either side of her while she drew us a picture on a scrap of butcher paper. Her dogs and cats came out so real you longed to pet them; you could see the breeze ruffling a hen's feathers. She'd learned to draw the animals in her father's corral on a fence board with a piece of charcoal. This was in the village of El Saúco, in the rainy, rocky north of Spain. Pepe Mendez, her second cousin, had walked over a mountain twenty miles away to ask for her hand in marriage. He was nineteen; she was six.

"You must have been darling!" Leticia and I cried, hopefully.

"I was skinny and ugly, like all children who lived through the war," Mama said. "But I had a third share of the land my brothers were going to inherit, and your father got along well with them."

Our parents' grocery store, Ultramarinos Mendez, on Esmeralda Street, sold not only Argentinean beef and fresh produce but Spanish imports—olive oil, canned sardines, dried garbanzos—to our homesick Spanish neighbors, who complained that garbanzos grown in Argentina had no flavor.

"Back in Spain, those dainty tongues were tasting thistles and boiled harnesses," Pepe said, but for family ears only. In the store, the customers were always right; at home, Leticia and I were. It was the classic story of immigrant parents slaving so their daughters could read novels in English at an expensive school. At eleven and twelve we were tall enough to look down at Mama's dandruff-flecked part— the secret to her shining hair was that she believed shampooing made you ill.

We hounded her for details of her courtship. "We were peasants," Mama said. "There were no ice cream parlors in El Saúco, no cinemas."

She didn't see much of Pepe during the years she was growing up. He was conscripted into the army, and after he returned home, he helped with the work on his own family's small plot. Then one day, her parents sent word that she was ready to be married.

"What made you decide you were ready to be married?"

"Well, I got my period."

Leticia and I shrieked and covered our ears. "You mean he *knew?* How could you ever face him?"

"That was how peasants thought. No man wanted a wife who couldn't bear children. And I was old—seventeen. I hadn't been able to eat meat because of the war."

In adolescence Leticia and I were mortified by our peasant mother—the circles of sweat under the arms of her blue work smock, the grunting noise she made cutting slices of serrano ham, the black gap where she'd had a tooth pulled. Her hair bunched in a fat knot like some greasy dead animal. At night my sister and I lay in bed together and discussed ways Mama could fix herself up, if she only cared to—she might be scrawny and dark, Leticia said, but so was Coco Chanel.

The good news for Leticia and me as teenagers was that we had absolute freedom. Our parents had no energy for discipline—they worked to pay for school fees, plaid jumpers, duffle coats, knee socks, bus passes out to the Anglo-Argentine suburb of Olivos, the realm of Miss Chandler. Rosa referred to her scornfully as Her Ladyship, but in fact she was a British former governess who'd established her school on the principle that the daughters of grocers were not inferior to the descendants of Argentina's founding fathers. To Miss Chandler, the only important hierarchy consisted of: 1. Shakespeare. 2. Wordsworth. 3. The Brontes.

Leticia and I flourished under her, one or the other of us always winning the year-end prizes for composition and recitation, our popularity enhanced by Leticia's beauty. I had inherited Pepe's bigger, blurrier features, as well as his tendency toward plumpness. I didn't much mind being the less-pretty sister—Victorian literature offers plenty of hope to plain, patient girls. I often opened conversations with, "About what you said yesterday—"

"Yesterday's just a song!" Leticia would say, laughing. In 1970 she was eighteen, and her long black hair fell just to the hem of her skirt. She was fearless: strolling into the most expensive downtown cafés and handing out stapled booklets of her poems, then looping back among the tables for donations. People gave her money—more, if they happened to glance in the booklet as well as gaze at those amazing legs.

At Buenos Aires University, Leticia had many admirers—*compañeros*, she called them. I wasn't entirely sure what that label entailed. Sometimes I accompanied her to the dingy cafes where she and her comrades sat for hours, debating politics. Cheap tobacco stung my eyes and rough red wine scoured my throat as I fought off a powerful sleepiness. It wasn't that I didn't care about social justice—but persuading those who didn't agree was hopeless. Privately, I saw the case for a kindly, well-educated dictator.

On nights when Leticia didn't include me, I'd go to pizzerias with my girlfriends or, occasionally, to the movies with some shy, sweaty-handed boy. But my favorite moment of any evening was when the *colectivo* lumbered to a stop on Esmeralda and the doors clattered open onto the street muffled in river fog. Leticia called me a little homebody, and it was true: even the creak and snap of the front gate latch filled me with happiness. Our parents slept like the dead, but I'd wait at the kitchen table, sipping strong maté until Leticia arrived.

One mauve almost-morning, I fluttered awake as she walked in, hair mussed and damp at the temples, cheeks flushed. "And what, exactly, have you been up to, young lady?" I asked her, in English. My imitation of Miss Chandler's spinsterish quaver was meant as a joke.

Leticia rolled her eyes. She kept her duffle coat on as she dumped spoon after spoon of sugar into the maté. Finally, she plopped into a chair and made the announcement that changed everything.

"Gabriel Baum wants to have coffee with you, Sonia."

It was the last thing I expected her to say. Of course I knew who Gabriel was: one of the *compañeros*, blond and a bit too good-looking. "Why?" I asked.

That wasn't exactly what I meant, but Leticia understood. "He saw you reading a book at a *colectivo* stop yesterday. He liked the look of you, he said. And you'd have reading in common—he wants to write for newspapers like his papa. Their apartment is stuffed with books."

"It was *The Mill on the Floss*," I said.

"If you marry him, you can frame the cover and hang it over your bed," Leticia said, and laughed when I reddened. "So I'll tell him yes?"

"No," I said. "He's stuck up." I gathered the maté gourd and teakettle and carried them to the sink. Pepe appeared in the kitchen, cinching his butcher's apron around his ever-expanding waist.

"Just off to bed, eh?" His tone was kindly. Neither he nor Mama would hear of us helping out in the grocery store. "How did you pass your evening, *queridas?*"

"Engaged in class struggle," Leticia said.

Two years later, *The Mill on the Floss* long forgotten on some cafe table, I had dinner with Gabriel and his parents. I was slim now, and for this event wore a blue and white checked miniskirt and beaded sandals, my dark hair parted in the middle. Increasingly, I was told that I resembled Leticia.

Walter Baum asked me if I was prepared to be a scribbler's wife. "We don't make much money," he said, though he was much more than a scribbler—in his study overlooking Bolivar Street, philosophical theories hatched and flew away across the ocean.

"When I get my degree, I'll be able to teach," I said. "Everybody wants English lessons nowadays."

Walter chuckled. "My dear, I did not think of that." His wife, Greta, smiled and patted my hand. They may be Germans, I thought, but they're not rigid or cold.

My parents, I believed, would have a different prejudice. The notion that the Catholic Mendezes might dare to condescend to the Jewish Baums infuriated me, as I dined on chicken marsala and asparagus with these soft-voiced, cultivated people in their tasteful, book-lined apartment.

Stuffed with books, Leticia had said once—she must have visited here. I pushed that thought aside in order to worry about how dinner between the prospective in-laws would go. I knew that Mama and Pepe would not speak during the meal—rural Spaniards consider talking while eating impolite. So they'd shovel their food, while the Baums sat, mildly puzzled, trying to introduce innocuous topics.

But it seemed that a wedding could not take place without this excruciating prelude.

Greta rose to clear the dishes, and I jumped up to help. I was thrilled when she entrusted me with the tray of coffee and strudel. After dessert, the men vanished into the blue smoke of Walter's study, and Greta brought out a scrapbook of cuttings she'd made of her husband's scholarly articles. The cities where they were published sounded like stops on the Orient Express: Venice, Budapest, Vienna, Paris, Prague, Frankfurt.

"Frankfurt is where I am from," Greta said, tenderly smoothing that page. "My entire family died in the camps."

I peered at the Frankfurt article, though I didn't know German.

"In English there's an expression—war stories," I told

Gabe, later that evening. "That's what our parents will talk about."

"Good, because I'm tired of being their only audience," he said. "You're lucky to have Leticia to share the burden." Naked, he got up from the bed and sat down at his desk chair and lit a cigarette.

"Won't your parents come in here if they smell smoke?"

"Never," Gabe said, beaming and glorious. His blond curls just brushed his shoulders.

We were in his bedroom, inches from Walter and Greta's heads resting on their pillows on the other side of the wall. Two hours earlier, Gabe had accompanied me down to the street, announcing to his parents that he'd see me home on the bus. Instead we'd gone to a café on the corner and drunk espressos until Gabe was reasonably sure Greta had finished putting away the silver and Walter had folded the damask tablecloth into a mathematically precise triangle. He did an impression of chain-smoking Walter huffing and whistling over this task.

"So what's your after-dinner job?" I'd asked. We were holding hands across the battered wooden table. I was dizzy with lust and caffeine.

"I am the entertainment," Gabe said.

"I'm afraid that won't be enough after we're married."

"Of course not, my love. After we're married, I shall fold the tablecloth."

"Fuck you," I said.

"On the contrary," he said sweetly. He held up his hand

for silence, as if he could actually hear Walter and Greta brushing their teeth, putting on their nightclothes, setting their folded eyeglasses on their bedside tables. "Now, the coast should be clear."

The precision of these arrangements led me to guess I wasn't the first girl Gabe had brought home after his parents were in bed. There was no practical reason to do this—the neighborhood around the university was dotted with by-the-hour hotels priced for student budgets.

Smoothing my hair in the elevator's beveled mirror, I saw my sister peering back at me. Then Gabe came into view, resting his chin on my head. "My father congratulated me," he said, smiling at our reflections. "He says I'm a lucky man."

"Well, he's right." So this was what it felt like to be Leticia, and desired.

Much later, and this time actually waiting for my *colectivo* on the corner of Bolivar and Belgrano, Gabe pulled me close for a kiss. "Did you ever sneak Leticia upstairs with you?" I blurted, surprising myself.

But here was the bus.

"I'll always love your sister," Gabe called, as I boarded. "If I hadn't known her, I wouldn't have met you."

"He's playing you, miss," the bus driver muttered. He pulled the door lever, slamming it.

Anyway, the Leticia Gabe had known and loved was no longer prancing around Buenos Aires selling poems in her little skirt. She'd moved out to the *campo*, to a commune on a dusty *estancia* with her new beau, Pedro Roth, a playwright.

Leticia had adopted Pedro's baggy, guerrilla-theatre getups as well as his solemn manner. Invited for a meatless *asado* one Saturday afternoon, Gabe murmured to me that somebody must have dripped the opposite of laughing gas into the lentils. "They're not Marxists—they're fucking Mennonites," he whispered, as I giggled helplessly.

To everyone's surprise, the Baum and Mendez parents got along beautifully, beginning with the dreaded engagement dinner. I'd instructed Pepe and Mama to take two bites and then say something—advice they followed precisely, like beginning swimmers taking breaths.

After the wedding, Gabe and I lived briefly with his parents on Bolivar Street, and he continued to behave as though we were teenagers getting away with something—cornering me behind doors and whispering dirty jokes at meals.

What our mothers had wanted all along were their lost families. So even after Gabe and I moved to a ground-floor apartment in the San Telmo district—midway between Ultramarinos Mendez and Bolivar Street—our mothers organized family fiestas for every Catholic and Jewish holiday that involved food. In addition, there were birthdays, as well as the baptism of the first granddaughter (Mari), and the bris of the first grandson (Julian).

Then came 1975, the year of funerals: first Pepe's in April (heart attack) and Walter's in December (lung cancer). Three months into 1976, the tottering government of Isabel Peron was overthrown in a military coup.

Winter ground on, gray and grim, and with it a flu that made the *colectivos* sound like rolling tubercular wards. I began walking everywhere with the children, past soldiers who held their machine gun barrels exactly at the height of Julian's head in his stroller.

The publisher of Gabe's newspaper was arrested, but over irregular financial dealings, Gabe assured me; nothing to do with the paper reporting disappearances.

"Nobody else is printing those stories," I said.

"Exactly," Gabe said. He drummed his fingers on the table.

I looked at him without speaking.

"Sonia, where could we go?" he said. Then he smiled. "There's no place on earth that would satisfy our mothers."

I've always thought of that as the last thing Gabe said to me: a little joke. Though when the police knocked on our door, the dishes were cleared and we were in pajamas, so we must have gone on talking.

The official who took down the report of my missing husband two days later commented that the playwright Pedro Roth had just reported the disappearance of his comrade, the poetess Leticia Mendez. "You ladies have the same surnames," he said. "You must be sisters. I hear she's pretty, too."

Not answering was also a reply, to which he nodded; he already had all the answers. Journalist Baum and Poetess Mendez were known leftists since their university days, he said—it was possible that they had gone into exile together.

A number of Argentinean subversives, he added, as I gripped the counter to stop the room from spinning, had been spotted sunning themselves on the beaches of Australia.

In exile myself in Maryland, I sometimes tried to imagine what it would be like if the police official were correct—if Gabe and Leticia were to appear on my doorstep in sunfaded beach togs, tanned and contrite, asking for my forgiveness. Long after I learned the truth—that my husband had been pushed, probably still alive, from a plane into the South Atlantic, and that my sister's bones had waited, jumbled up with hundreds of others, until DNA testing could be invented—this fantasy persisted. In it, I magnanimously invited the runaways in, offered them cold beer and sandwiches before asking the question I'd been puzzling over for years: *Why did you put me in the middle of the two of you?*

Meanwhile, I was in the middle of raising Mari and Julian in a brick townhouse in Bethesda. The human rights organization that had facilitated our fleeing Argentina had found me the apartment, as well as a job selling cosmetics at Saks Fifth Avenue, both of which I occupied for the next twenty-five years.

I refused to return to Buenos Aires, and during the long American summers, Mama would shutter the store on Esmeralda Street and fly north to help with the children. I'd come home at the end of the day to chaos. The living room draped in sheets for a circus tent; sofa cushions piled in the kitchen for a fort, at which clementine peels had been flung; more groceries scattered around the dining room, where they'd been playing at Granny's Store in Argentina. Mama, like the children, might be wearing elements of various Halloween costumes, brandishing a wand like some spidery, gray-haired fairy.

I'd take a deep breath. "Looks like everybody's been having fun."

"They were very good," Mama invariably said, hugging her glamorous grandchildren to her, as if they'd all won Oscars. Unbelievable, I'd fume later, to Gabe, to whom I still spoke— sometimes aloud—when I was alone and despairing. His eloquent silence forced me to amend: *Of course I'm glad Mama's finally able to show affection, that the children love her.* During the last weeks of every school year, they'd be crossing off the calendar days until Granny's plane landed.

One afternoon ten years into my exile, a rumpled-looking man in a tweed jacket approached my counter. I smiled encouragingly—I was used to men mumbling the ridiculous name of a lipstick from a scrap of paper, filling a shopping order for a wife or girlfriend.

"Can I help you, sir?" Our eyes met. "Pedro Roth. *Dios mío.*"

"Only yesterday I learned you were in America, Sonia."

In a dark restaurant a block from Sak's, Pedro told me that he'd been hauled off a bus and arrested the day after reporting my sister's disappearance. He'd never seen her again. But he'd been with Gabe: in the basement of a building somewhere in downtown Buenos Aires. Into their converted prison came the sounds of traffic, a knife-grinder's whistle, even the shouts of schoolchildren. "I thought, why do we hear street noises, and yet nobody out there hears us screaming?" Pedro said. "I decided that we were already dead, and this was Hell."

I looked down at my enormous, untouched hamburger. "Did Gabe say—"

"Sonia, there was nothing like conversation in that place."

One night, Gabe and some others had been loaded onto a truck and taken away. Days later, another group went. Then another, and another.

"The death flights happened on Thursdays," I said. "That came out in the military trials—that they were on a schedule."

"I didn't even know if Thursday still existed," Pedro said.

It had also been night when he was taken out, alone. Riding across miles of windswept pampas he'd braced himself for some particularly grisly fate. Instead, he'd been let go in the middle of a field of sheep. "'Tell your friends at Amnesty that sometimes we are *buenos*,'" they'd told him, laughing and spitting.

Now he had a teaching job at Georgetown. He was married to a former student named Helen. They had a child, Joaquin.

"Didn't your in-laws think that was an alarming resume?" I said. "From prisoner to college professor?"

"They'd written letters on my behalf to Amnesty," Pedro

said. "So did Helen, along with the rest of her high school Spanish class. The world is the size of a handkerchief, Sonia, and yet you found a corner of it to hide in." He reached out and held my wrist gently, as if taking my pulse. "You're so like Leticia."

"I'd like to meet your family," I said. I never did.

It seems inaccurate to call what happened between Pedro and me over the next several years a love affair, though there was the secrecy, and sometimes, the desperation. But I never expected or wanted him to leave Helen for me. Wasn't there enough destruction on this planet? Also, I'd been out of Argentina long enough to be impatient with our particular nationality's brand of male preening. Of course, Gabe had had that insatiable vanity, too, if I remembered hard enough. My Iranian friend, Azin, and I used to chuckle over our perfect disappeared husbands, who never farted or dropped a sock.

When Pedro called me at work and said he had to see me, my colleagues loyally covered, and I went. We'd linger over coffee or if the weather was fine stroll along the Potomac— so like, and yet unlike, the River Plate at home. At some point one or the other of us would suggest "stopping to rest,"—as if it were an afterthought. Pedro had a friend who was seldom in Washington, and had entrusted him with the keys to his apartment.

"He's Argentinean, no doubt," I said. "The way you stick together."

"The way we stick together," Pedro agreed, smiling—

Leticia and I had known him forever. He'd attended the boys' school down the block from Miss Chandler's. A chubby, untidy child—beneath the notice of the Mendez sisters, Pedro now claimed: "It was always the pair of you, heads together like Siamese twins, whispering secrets."

And yet, I hadn't known that she'd slept with him in high school—"out of monumental pity," Pedro said. He recited the last poem Leticia had been working on until I learned it, too. We agreed that it should always be memorized, never written down.

The bed in that apartment was a daybed pushed under a window, and we'd open the blinds and lie flat like a pair of paper dolls as we talked and watched the sky, which shifted through the seasons from deep, wintry blue to hazy summer white. It could have been the sky in Argentina; the stars were different here, but we never had rendezvous at night.

Each time, before leaving, we'd drink maté, using the gourd and electric kettle that the (obviously) Argentinean friend kept in his tiny kitchen. Once I brought a packet of imported biscuits I'd found in a deli, and when Pedro bit into one, his eyes filled with tears. We hadn't wept when speaking of the dead, but now we were howling over stale crackers baked in Buenos Aires.

"Mind we don't leave crumbs," Pedro said finally, and I, the Argentinean female, scurried to find a broom and dustpan.

I believe, to this day, that our families never knew about us—though sometimes, in summer when Mama was babysitting, I'd come home from work to find my dresser riffled through, as if I were a schoolgirl suspected of hiding contraband. But Pedro and I wrote no love letters, sent no texts or emails, never exchanged gifts. It was a relationship that could easily be disappeared.

Which was what I did to it. I'd stopped for Pedro and his family by chance at a downtown crosswalk. He didn't notice me—he didn't drive, and had never ridden in my car.

I'd always pictured his wife, Helen, with one of those blank, smiley American faces—a cartoon American—but now I saw in her vivid, intelligent expression a woman I'd probably like. And it was clear that Pedro liked her, the way he was leaning toward her, touching her arm as he spoke. I decided I was glad of that—mostly.

Behind them trailed their twelve-year-old, Joaquin. He was several years younger than my Julian, just on the edge of that stage of wary, sullen bravado. If asked, he'd have said he didn't give a crap about what his dad did in his spare time. That was what froze my heart.

What I'd missed, in my obsession with secrecy, were my children's secrets. When had the Mendez-Baum house become the high school party house? One night I came home from work to unfamiliar odors, a living room filled with suspiciously merry teenagers. Mama, supposedly chaperoning, was in the kitchen, watching her soaps on Telemundo. "You and Leticia ran wild in Buenos Aires," she said. "And yet you survived."

"One of us did." I called parents to come fetch their high and drunken offspring, then went upstairs to bathe and weep and complain to my murdered husband.

Suddenly I felt calm, knowing what I had to do. I dressed and went back to the living room, where Mari and Julian were meekly cleaning up the mess.

"Sit, both of you," I said. "There are a few things you need to hear."

I told them about the nights of political debate in the university cafe where I'd first noticed their father. I described the coup, the machine guns pointed at Julian's downy head, the unmarked Ford Falcons nosing along our street at dusk, Gabe's newspaper articles about the disappearances, the silent policemen who waited while he put on a coat and tie for his interrogation. I told them that an old friend of ours, Pedro Roth, had gotten in touch, and had filled me in on details of the secret prison next to a schoolyard, the military planes that dumped evidence of torture into freezing water.

"Papi was in the Navy Mechanics' School prison?" Julian said finally. "That's so crazy. We studied about it in Spanish class."

Mari came over and put her arms around me. She still smelled of some sweet, alcoholic mixture. "Poor Mama, how awful for you."

"I hope that Pedro Roth won't be lurking around all the time now," my mother called, from the other room. "I never liked him. Whatever did Leticia see in him?"

"He won't," I said.

* * *

Greta died and left the Bolivar Street apartment to me. It was an unusable bequest, since I wouldn't return there, and would never sell it. With her old friend gone, Mama sold the shop on Esmeralda Street for a tidy sum and moved permanently to the United States to live with me.

"You'll kill each other," Mari and Julian predicted, smiling grimly. They were out of college, with their own apartments, though neither offered to take Granny in and avert the bloodbath. But it helped that I was at work all day, giving Mama the freedom to putter around the house, poke through drawers and medicine cabinets and dust spots I'd missed. Every afternoon, she'd walk to the supermarket to buy fresh vegetables for our supper.

What I didn't know was that she was getting lost on the way home.

Every day for the past two weeks, according to the Spanish-speaking policeman I encountered drinking lemonade in my kitchen.

I walked him to the front door. He was a sweet, moon-faced kid, his singsong Cuban accent so broad I wanted to laugh. "Your mom said she was afraid to be alone, so I told her I'd wait a couple minutes until you got here."

Rosa, afraid? I couldn't imagine her saying the word. I thanked him again and went back to the kitchen, where her soap opera was just beginning.

My mother glanced up from the TV. "Isn't he a handsome young fellow? I thought you'd like him."

I laughed then. "He's Julian's age, Mama!"

She shrugged. "You've kept your looks, Sonia. That cop was telling me Miami is lovely this time of year." She gestured toward the TV. "And here they are advertising package vacations. Are you still afraid to fly?"

I felt the soft, damp embrace of Miami the minute we stepped onto the jetway. Rosa walked ahead of me, talking and shaking her head.

Struggling behind with the hand luggage, I called, "I can't hear what you're saying."

She raised her voice, but kept going. "I said, 'You ought to have thanked me, Sonia, for treating you to this vacation.'"

"But we haven't even—well, thank you for inviting me."

"My daughter is only grateful when I demand it," she said to the air in front of her. She stopped, turned, and disappeared. There was a little scream, a horrible cracking sound.

She was lying on the ground below a short flight of steps, moaning—which was actually good, a Cuban man from the plane said—it meant that she wasn't losing consciousness. He knelt beside Mama and took her other hand calmly, as if he'd dealt with similar accidents before.

While she was being lifted on a stretcher, he gave me his card. "Please call if there's anything I can do."

I looked up at him. He was heavyset like Mama's policeman, gray-haired, but with lovely long-lashed black eyes. Mario Gutierrez, Realtor, the card said, and then in Spanish: *Agente inmobilario.*

"Not a great moment in Florida for the profession, but at least I've been able to catch up on my reading," he said with the cheerful air of someone who says the same things often.

I set Mario Gutierrez' card on the mantel of the condo's fake fireplace, though I couldn't think of a reason to call him.

After a week in the hospital with a broken hip, Mama was moved for rehab to a nursing home in Coconut Grove. Every morning, I drove my rental car along the Dixie Highway to the facility. The Spanish-speaking nurses appeared to find Mama delightful. *La condesa,* they called her, the countess: with her continental accent and aquiline features, her thick white hair in an aristocratic chignon.

In the dayroom, doing occupational therapy, she drew portraits of long-dead pets from photographs, charming the other old women. The few old men in the place all appeared to be in love with her. "Rose, hey there, Rose," they'd call from their parked wheelchairs, as she advanced with slow, regal steps down the corridors.

"I want to stay here, with my new friends," she announced, after the bone doctor gave her permission to fly home. "I've got the money to pay for it."

I drove back to the condo in the gathering dusk and then walked out across the cooling sand to the water's edge, discussing the matter with Gabe. If I sold the Maryland townhouse I could buy a place here, in the depressed Florida market, and have something left over. Mari and Julian would be pleased by the idea of a beach crash pad, and equally pleased that I wasn't constantly dropping in on them—evidently, daily visits to adult children aren't an American custom.

I could finish my college degree, give English classes to the nurses, reread *Wuthering Heights*, grow lemons and gardenias on my balcony. The rattle of palmetto leaves and the whoosh of sliding glass doors would become the new sounds of homecoming. The ocean lapping at my feet was the same water that had touched Gabe's body, somewhere over the blurred purple edge of the horizon.

I even know a realtor, I said aloud. I've got his business card.

I never believed that Gabe was an actual ghost—a being whose existence would survive me. Talking to him was a habit, a comfort, a door to my past.

And as I stood ankle-deep in balmy water, it was as if the door opened wide—to reveal Buenos Aires boulevards and the gleaming monuments of Washington, the odors of perfume and diesel fumes and Spanish *chorizo* and tear gas, the snap of the gate latch at Ultramarinos Mendez and the creak of the daybed under the window.

Then I pictured something that had not yet happened: myself unlocking the door on Bolivar Street, the parquet creaking under my feet, the worn damask chairs, the cobwebbed piles of books. A tall, solid presence beside me, setting down our luggage, remarking how much morning light these rooms must get, in a lilting island accent that made me smile.

Call him, Sonia. I am quite sure I heard this.

116

Teardown

While Mari and Brian were waiting for the house they'd bought in suburban Maryland to be torn down and replaced, they offered to let Julian stay there. He wouldn't even have to mow the lawn: Everything Must Go.

"So if you don't mind living with uncertainty," Mari told him. Julian had been sleeping on the sofa bed in their mother's tiny apartment since getting out of the hospital a month earlier.

"I love Uncertainty," Julian said. "She leaves wet towels on the floor and dishes in the sink, but she's amazing in bed."

Mari looked stern. "You'll be living among our future neighbors," she said. "No funny business."

Before marrying Brian, Julian thought, his sister would have laughed at his joke, and they'd have reminisced about some of the parties they'd had in high school.

Brian drove Julian and his few boxes of possessions to the teardown, where they set up one of the empty bedroom with a futon, a floor lamp and an ancient TV with a video player built into it.

"You're lucky," Brian said. "We put all this junk out for the Salvation Army, but it rained so they never came."

"I'm lucky the stuff dried off," Julian said, and smiled. He often played a little game where he smiled whenever his brother-in-law said something that proved what a jerk he was. Since Julian smiled so much when they were together, he assumed Brian thought they were friends.

"You're not going to get reception without cable," Brian said, fiddling with the TV's rabbit ears. "And where are you going to get videos anymore?"

"I've got some good porn on video," Julian said.

Brian looked startled, as if his four-year-old had said this. "You'll close the window blinds, there, buddy?"

"Sure thing," Julian said, grinning wildly.

After Brian left, Julian strolled through the empty, dusty rooms. The bare walls made a refreshing change from his mother's place, where photos of him and Mari at adorable ages oppressed him everywhere he looked.

As often seemed to happen, thinking of his mother made her appear. Sonia de Baum was on the front stoop ringing the doorbell, wearing a white lab coat with "Sonia" stitched on the pocket. Back in Argentina, she'd been an English teacher, but when she came to the U.S. twenty-five years ago she got a temporary job in the cosmetics department at Saks and never left. Her heavy accent was an asset there, where the saleswomen's voices evoked the exotic beauty of foreign cities: Tehran, Moscow, Buenos Aires. Julian was only three when his family fled. He worked as a translator, and his English had no perceptible accent.

"I got you a few groceries, *hijo,*" Sonia said, tilting her cheek for a kiss. In addition to roasted chickens, deli salads, gallons of milk and juice, she'd bought chips, salsa and a couple of six-packs of beer.

"A few groceries?" Julian laughed.

"You could invite your high school friends over," Sonia said. She looked at him hopefully.

Julian imagined calling them. *Hey, I just got out of the loony bin—let's party!* "When I think of all the times you tried to *prevent* me having parties," he said.

"That was then," she said. "Your papá will be pleased to hear that you're feeling better and living in a nice house."

"Give him my love," Julian said as she left.

He couldn't really remember his father, though as a child he sometimes overheard his mother talking to him in her bedroom. But whenever Julian opened the door, only Sonia was there. This was because his father, Gabriel Baum, was a *desaparecido,* a disappeared person.

Night fell, and Julian decided it was dinnertime. He opened the refrigerator, but making a choice seemed daunting. He retrieved a beer and went into the bedroom and dug out his video. *Teen House Party,* it was called—a college girlfriend had given it to him as a joke years ago. The porn actors were hilariously beyond their teens, but the hostess of the party, "Shelly," was pretty and had a trace of acting talent.

He fell asleep before the tape ended, and the great thing was that when he woke up the next morning he knew exactly who and where he was.

Six months earlier, in the D.C. apartment where he was living with his girlfriend, Alison, Julian was sitting at his computer when he heard a siren. He glanced up to see an ambulance careening along Columbia Road. When he looked back at the screen, he suddenly couldn't decipher the English on the page he was translating. He wandered around his living room, disoriented, examining the books, furniture and framed Smithsonian art exhibit posters for clues as to where he was. Then he heard a key scrape in the lock of the front door. A blond woman in blue scrubs entered.

"*Hola*," he said.

"*Hola*, Julian," she replied gamely.

"Who are you?" Julian asked in Spanish.

The woman studied him for a long moment. "I'm calling a taxi, Julian," she said calmly, keeping her eyes on him as she pulled a cell phone from her purse. "I thought we could visit a friend of mine."

At the hospital, Alison's "friend" gave him an injection of sedatives, and the next morning he was himself again. The psychiatrist Julian consulted at Alison's insistence told him that temporary amnesia was a normal response to trauma—

even forgotten trauma, such as his father's arrest. It had been nearly 30 years since the secret police had come to the Baums' Buenos Aires apartment in the middle of the night. And although Julian supposedly had slept through the ordeal, the sirens on Columbia Road might have awakened a memory.

Julian met a few times with the shrink. His little "episode," the doctor said, might recur decades from now, or never.

Julian took a notebook from his pocket. "So what does Wednesday afternoon thirty years from now look like?" he asked, and the doctor laughed.

"You've snowed him, Julian," Alison said. "Find another doctor."

He didn't, and Alison's doubt of his sanity became a sort of background humming noise in the apartment. It was similar to the vibration you got from a woman who's been cheated on, but this Julian hadn't done.

* * *

Wearing only his boxers, Julian went to the kitchen and boiled water for instant coffee. He carried it through the sliding glass door to the back patio. Over a hedge on one side of the yard he saw a woman with curly brown hair doing what seemed to be a set of bending and stretching exercises. He strolled over and peered across the hedge. "Oh, you're picking tomatoes," he said amiably.

The woman appeared to assess him. "And you're going to take some." Her small, compact face was freckled; she had small, high breasts under a running top, and wiry, freckled arms. "You must be Mr. Hartford. I've met your wife, and your darling son."

"Please call me Julian," he said. "And excuse my attire."

"Not a problem. I'm Shelly."

"That's easy to remember."

"Really? Why?"

"An old friend's name," Julian said. "I always wondered what became of her."

"Well, your wife is lovely. I've been defending her to people in the neighborhood who are not happy about the teardown. 'So what if they're ruining the roofline to put up their McMansion,' I tell them. 'She's very nice.' "

"It might not be a teardown," Julian said. "I've kind of moved in by myself to see how it would work as is."

Shelly nodded. "Renovations are very stressful on a marriage." A breeze blew her hair about her shoulders. She looked more attractive than she had at first. "So is turning forty." She gave him a wry smile. "You'll never guess where my forty-year-old husband is." He shook his head. "Mongolia."

"Wow," Julian said.

"On a dig. He said it's always been his dream. Sounds more like a nightmare, I said. And I get to stay behind and make tomato confit. So dig that."

"What's confit?"

"It's like jam. You cook the hell out of it, but it's salty."

"Sounds awful."

"It's not bad. You spread it on slices of baguette. It's very popular. If you came over later, you could try some."

"All right."

"Say fiveish? Should I call you to confirm?"

"I'll just come. I don't have a phone."

"Why not?"

"I dropped it on the sidewalk." Julian wasn't about to explain that he'd dropped it from the roof of a building, causing a crowd to gather.

"I'd die without my phone," Shelly said cheerfully. "When you get a new one, I'm listed under my maiden name. Shelly Snow."

Julian had just returned to the kitchen with his hands full of tomatoes when his sister and his nephew walked in the front door without knocking. Well, it was Mari's house. Danny ran to him. "The bulldozers are coming, Uncle Julian!" he shouted.

"Not today, Sweetie," Mari said. She was carrying a man's gray suit on a hanger.

"The house is mine now," Julian growled. "All mine!" He laughed maniacally and grabbed Danny, who shrieked with terrified delight, and flipped him over his shoulder. Danny was Julian's godson, and Julian had occasional fantasies about becoming his male guardian— helping a divorced or widowed Mari raise him.

She handed him the suit. "I hope you remember you have a job interview today at five-thirty."

"Right," Julian said. "I mean, of course I remember."

He went into the bedroom to try on the suit. His interview was for a translation gig with one of Brian's law partners. The only qualification Julian lacked was a suit, so he was borrowing one of Brian's.

"This'll do OK," Julian called through the door. Mari knocked and came in.

"Just OK? *Hermanito,* you look fantastic. I always thought you and Brian were the same size." She came over and patted his back, his shoulders, his arms. "You're exactly the same size."

"I don't see why he'd give this to the Salvation Army."

"What Salvation Army? That's one of his best suits, made to measure."

"Oh," Julian said.

Mari scowled. "He wouldn't give you a garbage suit to wear to an interview."

"Did I say it was garbage?"

"Why are you so obnoxious to him all the time? He says you smile condescendingly when he tries to have a conversation with you. When he came home from helping you move, he was almost in tears about it."

"Oh, God," Julian said. He sat down on the futon.

"Look at it from his perspective. He marries me, and he gets an Argentinean mother-in-law who talks to her dead husband, and you, who tried to jump off the top of your apartment building, sneering at him for helping you get back on your feet."

Julian rested his forehead on his bent knees. He took a

deep breath, and looked up into Mari's face. "For the last time—I wasn't going to jump off my building. I was just sitting on the roof, thinking. Then my phone fell out of my pocket and someone on the street called 911."

"OK," Mari said. "I shouldn't have said that." She knelt and held out her arms. "Friends?"

Julian allowed her to hug him. "I met your neighbor, Shelly Snow, today," he said. "She invited me over for tomato confit."

"I hope you're not going," Mari said.

"I can't. I have this job interview."

"You shouldn't go any time. That woman has ants in her pants. I felt like she was coming on to *me*."

He laughed. "She said confit, not condoms."

"We're going to be living next door, Julian. It could get awkward. It's bad enough that you seduced all my friends."

"Only what, three. And that was high school. Compared to most men my age, I'm a monk."

"Monkey is more like it. So stop it before it starts, Mr. Dimples and Eyelashes."

She stood up and smoothed her hair in the closet mirror, where her own considerable dimples and eyelashes were reflected.

"I wouldn't have sex with her," Julian said. "She's weird. She thinks I'm your husband, even though we almost look like twins."

Mari whirled around and stared at him. "You told her that?" she cried. "I guess you think it's a great joke for her to believe she's hitting on Brian. What has he ever done to make you hate him so much?"

Julian shrugged. "I just miss the way you used to be."

"Grow up, Julian. Only a loser wants to be sixteen forever."

Tears started in his eyes. The only time he ever cried was when he fought with his sister. "*Jodete,*" he said hoarsely.

Mari stomped out, slamming the bedroom door. Through the thin wall separating his room from the living room he heard Danny: "What did Uncle Julian do, Mommy?"

"He said a bad word. And now he has to stay in his room."

It was ten minutes till five. Standing on Shelly Snow's front porch, peering through the screen door, Julian could see the coffee table set with an open bottle of wine, two glasses, a plate of sliced bread and a dish of what looked like jam. Bossa nova music floated in the air. He had just turned to go back down the porch steps when Shelly appeared. She was wearing a tomato-colored halter dress.

"Punctual! I like that." She held the screen door open, and a wave of perfume hit him. "Don't you look dapper," she said. "You'll have to be careful not to spill any confit on that suit." She handed him a glass of white wine. "I saw your wife drive away pretty fast a little bit ago. Is everything OK?"

"Everything's great." He hesitated. "Actually, Mari's my sister."

"I am so glad to hear that! I've heard that's happening a lot in the recession—grown siblings living together. Well, come sit down."

"Actually, I can't stay. I have a job interview that I forgot about."

"A job interview now?" Shelly said, skeptical. "You say 'actually' a lot, you know that?" She took the still-full wineglass from him. "At least confit doesn't go bad."

Her hurt tone implied that this was merely the last in a long list of instances where Julian had disappointed her. He thought that if he hadn't had the fight with Mari and the pending interview he might have slept with her.

"Maybe we could do this another time," he said.

"Maybe." She stared at the floor.

He hated to walk out without her even looking at him. "I appreciate you inviting me, Shelly," he said.

"You're forgiven," he heard her say softly, as the screen door closed behind him.

It was only five-fifteen when Julian reached the lobby of the hotel where his potential boss had arranged to meet him. He decided he needed that untouched glass of wine to steady his nerves, so he went into the hotel bar and ordered the house white. A slender young woman with straight, fair hair sat down on the stool beside his. She was wearing a flowered, summery dress.

"There you are," she said.

"Here I am," Julian said, playing along.

"You're younger and thinner than you look in your picture."

"You know what they say about photography."

"Do I look like what you expected?"

This allowed him to turn and gaze into her pale blue eyes. "Even prettier," Julian said, though he knew he shouldn't. Her real date was likely to arrive at any moment.

"You're very kind. I'm wiped. That wine looks delicious, by the way." She waved to the bartender and pointed to Julian's glass. "I got in this morning from Buenos Aires."

Was *she* playing *him*? "What were you doing there?" he asked cautiously.

"Oh, the usual. I could tell they didn't expect me to be a woman, though they were all very polite, complimenting my Spanish. So the contract negotiations were a breeze. Everyone went home rich and happy, and I ended up with three days to explore the city. I loved it, Larry."

"What did you love about it?"

"Buenos Aires? It was beautiful. All those grand old buildings, the jacaranda trees, the boulevards, the cafés. The people are so lively and charming. The men sort of hassle you, but I could handle them. The city's like Paris, only more so. Who knew?"

Julian hardly dared breathe. "I'm from Buenos Aires," he said.

"What? You never said."

Just then, a man approached them. He was dressed for an evening out, in a sport coat and open-necked white shirt. His eyes and hair were brown. He and Julian didn't really look alike, though perhaps they could have been selected for the same police lineup.

"You must be Samantha," the man said, and held out his hand. "I'm Larry."

Samantha turned toward him and took his hand wordlessly. Julian couldn't see her face.

"Sorry I'm late. The traffic from the airport was unbelievable." He looked at Julian. "Glad you found someone to keep you company."

"Larry, this is…," Samantha said.

"Julian," Julian said. Larry nodded, but said nothing.

"Julian's from Argentina," Samantha said.

"That's a long trip," Larry said. "What brings you to America?"

"A job interview," Julian said.

"You know, I don't really see how they're going to solve the immigration issue. It's a huge problem, but nobody knows how to fix it."

"It's not very nice to say Julian's a problem, Larry," Samantha said.

"I didn't mean him specifically. He's obviously fluent in English and has a real job interview and everything. I was speaking in general terms. Well, it was great to meet you. We should get going, though, Samantha. I made dinner reservations."

"Wait, Larry. I've been trying to tell you something. Julian's—he's an old friend from college. He went back to Buenos Aires after we graduated, and we've just bumped into each other, in this bar. Isn't that amazing?"

"You went to Stanford?" Larry said to Julian. "What year'd you graduate?"

"Two thousand," Julian said. He shook his head. "It's hard to believe."

"I'm UVA ninety myself," Larry said. "Then I stuck around for law school."

"Wow," Julian said.

"Wouldn't it be nice if Julian joined us for dinner, Larry?" Samantha said.

Larry looked aghast. "Samantha, I flew all this way to see you! It was not easy to get away," he added more quietly, as if whomever he'd gotten away from was lurking nearby.

"I know. But I told you I wanted to take things slowly. We can all three have dinner tonight. Then tomorrow you and I will go see your ancestor's signature on the Declaration of Independence."

Larry sighed. He gave Samantha a long look, and then smiled faintly. Something about that smile made Julian think that Larry had kids. "I'll tell you what," he said finally. "Why don't you and your college friend have dinner tonight, and I'll call for you tomorrow."

Julian thought you had to admire someone who could master himself so completely after what was clearly a blow. "Is nine o'clock too early?"

"Perfect." Samantha put both her hands in Larry's and kissed his cheek. "It's wonderful to finally see you in person."

"Same. Well, have a nice dinner. I'm going to stay here and have a very uncollegiate martini."

"Goodbye, Larry," Julian said.

"Good luck," Larry said.

Samantha and Julian walked silently through the hotel lobby to the street. They'd gone a block before he spoke.

"That was amazing, Samantha."

"Yes, well, I didn't care for the way he treated you. What if you were my friend from Stanford?" She turned to face him. Now her eyes were cold steel. "What exactly were you playing at in there?

"I know I shouldn't have pretended to be Larry. But there was something about you. I didn't want you to disappear."

"And you aren't really from Buenos Aires, are you?"

"I really am."

She snorted. "I don't think so. Prove it. What street did you live on?"

"I don't remember." All at once, though, he could see it: a row of sycamores in the slanting southern light, steps leading to a heavy wooden door, scampering to keep up with striding trouser legs. His father's? "I was three when we left."

"And you never went back?"

"My mother never wanted to."

Samantha's nose wrinkled. "This is beginning to smell like bullshit. Why didn't you go back? Argentina's a fabulous place."

"We left during the dirty war," Julian said. "My father was a journalist who became a *desaparecido*." He and Samantha were walking along dusky residential streets now, turning corners in unspoken concert, as you did on a Ouija board. "My mother worried she'd disappear, too, or that we'd be kidnapped. So we went into hiding in other people's houses. But they became afraid to have us, and so we escaped to Uruguay, and then we came here."

They'd reached a small park, and Samantha sat down on a bench. "I guess I believe you," she said.

Julian sat beside her, not too close. He wanted Samantha to believe he was an Argentinean, but not a hassling one.

"Did you ever find out what happened to your father?" she said.

"Years later. He was taken up in a military plane and pushed into the ocean. They did that to people they tortured, who were too messed up to let go. A friend of my mother's who'd been in prison with him saw him being taken out to the airstrip."

Samantha moaned and buried her face in her hands. "That's so horrible," she said. "Your own dad."

"When I was little, I thought 'disappeared' meant he was like a magician," Julian said. "My sister and I were in high school when we learned the whole truth. It was horrible, like you said, but it was also like hearing about the death of a saint, or Martin Luther King—someone historical. But then a few months ago, things started to get strange. Like I'd be doing a Spanish translation and forget how to speak English. Or I'd find myself going up to high places and leaning over, trying to imagine what my dad felt before he died. I did that on the roof of my building, and the paramedics came and I ended up in the hospital. Even my girlfriend thought I was trying to kill myself. But I really don't think I was."

"So did your girlfriend bail on you?"

"I don't blame her. She's a nurse. She takes care of sick people all day as it is." He met Samantha's gaze. "I guess we're not going to have dinner," he said.

"No. I've got an early start tomorrow."

"Are you really going out with Larry? What is he, married?"

She sighed. "Men! He's widowed, and his sister moved in to help with his kids. But she's a little controlling, so it's rough. I met him at an online professional forum, and then we got to chatting offline." She gave him a sharp look. "You may have had tragedy in your life, Julian, but you shouldn't have lied to me."

"Maybe Larry's lying to you, too."

"He's not," she said, shaking her head vigorously. "I'm a lawyer. I can tell when people are lying." She flushed. "Usually."

"I promise, Samantha, that's the last time I'll ever lie to you. Could I please see you again?"

"I'm busy this weekend. Then I'm going on another business trip."

"Could I call you? Or e-mail you?"

"No. No e-mail. Give me your phone number, and I'll think about it and maybe call you."

"I don't have a phone at the moment. But now I have a reason to get one."

Giving Samantha his mother's number would make him seem pathetic. And Mari would probably warn Samantha away from him. "Maybe you could call my neighbor, Shelly

Snow. She's listed. She's a little peculiar, but I think she'd take a message."

"Shelly Snow. That's easy to remember."

"Could I see you back to the hotel?"

"I'd rather walk by myself. I'll be fine."

"I'm sure you will." He held out his hand, and she shook it. "I really, really hope I hear from you, Samantha."

"Goodbye, Julian."

It wasn't until he was back at the house that he remembered his job interview. Christ! But maybe it was for the best. He'd have the suit cleaned, and send flowers to show Mari and Brian how sorry he was about everything. Then he'd find a job without their help. He'd spend more quality time with his mother, get his life together. He was thirty; it was time.

Julian was sitting on the edge of the futon, still wearing the handsome bespoke suit, when he put his video in. The truth was that the old tape wasn't all that erotic. Often he'd only watch the opening scene, when Shelly is dressing for her party, setting out refreshments, smiling at her reflection in the mirror. There was something in her sweet, earnest expression that beguiled him, though he knew the porn actress was probably washed up or dead by now, and probably not even named Shelly. But insofar as you could love someone who never spoke to you, never answered you or argued, it could be said that what he felt for her was a kind of love.

Why else would he sit in an empty, doomed house and quietly ask, "So what do you think, Shell? Do you think she'll call?"

Buenos Aires, 1984

Isabel Conde pushed open the window of the airport bus and inhaled the familiar autumn smells of woodsmoke, grilled meat, diesel, burnt sugar. All up and down Avenida de Mayo, vendors were selling candy and flowers at stoplights—that was new, since the arrival of democracy, as were the women her mother's age wearing blue jeans on the street.

In the seat beside Isa, her boyfriend, Richard, was reading a guidebook. She'd teased him when he bought it, though in fact she wasn't being very helpful about pointing out landmarks.

Instead she was gazing out the window at her old neighborhood, Barrio Norte, which she hadn't seen in six years. During that time there'd been a military dictatorship, a war with England and a presidential election, and yet nothing here looked different: the same expensive shops selling bed linens, cutlery, hand-smocked children's clothes, the same plush, quiet cafes. The smashed windows of the Banco Espiritu Santo had been replaced.

"The Bank of the Holy Spirit," Richard said, looking up from his book. "Where would Jesus bank?"

Isa smiled but didn't reply.

She could have told him that she'd been at the student protest that broke the glass, but the old habit of silence had taken over. Even in her father's Renault, as he'd driven her to the airport six years earlier, they'd said nothing. On her lap was her mother's mink coat—wildly inappropriate for the midwestern college student she was about to become. Her cousin Hector a *desaparacido*, Isa was being spirited out of the country with the help of a former colleague of her father's who taught at a small college in St. Paul, Minnesota. Once there, Isa had sold the coat and bought a down jacket, heavy boots and dungarees, as well as a term's worth of books.

But at the airport, she'd slung the fur over one shoulder and given her father a jaunty little wave—as if leaving Argentina had been her idea, not his.

Her parents didn't visit her. Once a semester a check made out to the college arrived; Isa made up the difference with student loans and waitressing. Still, every letter from her mother contained a reference to how much she was costing them.

But now Isa had her teaching credential and could feed herself as well as Richard, who was in dental school. Two weeks earlier, he'd surprised her with a diamond ring as they walked beside Lake Harriet. He was a kind, practical man who'd decided on dentistry partly because dentists, like teachers, can take long vacations. His idea was that they'd spend their summers fishing, camping and canoeing on the northern lakes. Eventually, they could move up to Duluth or Bemidji, to a cabin where they'd hear wolves and loons and read Russian novels under heavy quilts. Isa believed her family would find choosing to live in the forest incomprehensible. They'd take in Richard's easy, open manners, her flashy ring, and conclude that she was marrying a *yanqui* straight out of a movie. Their dismissal would probably cause her to love him more.

At Calle Austria she pressed the stop bell and motioned to Richard that they should descend. "Do we go out the back door?" he called.

"Yeah."

"OK, you grab this bag and I'll get the backpacks."

He seemed unaware that this exchange had caught the attention of the entire bus. Isa didn't see anyone she recognized, and yet everyone looked familiar—elderly men wearing neckties with cardigans, haughty, lovely schoolgirls in plaid jumpers. Isa had once thought her school uniform would be a perfect disguise—in it, she'd convey messages between Hector and his *compañeros*.

But now she and Richard were being minutely observed: their slangy English, baggy Levis and clownish running shoes. *Foreign hippies—they'll be infesting Buenos Aires now that the generals are gone.* Isa felt these thoughts emanating from a woman sitting opposite the door, her large, stiff handbag perched on her knees like a lapdog.

Fuck off, fascist cow.

"Which way?" Richard said, and it struck her that the sight of the cafe on the corner meant nothing to him, nor the *papelería* where her sister, Mayte, used to take her to buy school supplies, nor the uneven cobbles where their heels would skid, coming home late from a party. Richard knew every inch of her body, but he couldn't stroll casually into her head like the purse lady had done. She suddenly felt desolate, and as they climbed the steps of her parents' building, she wished that she were alone.

Amanda, the concierge, was polishing the elevator brasses. She dropped her rag and hugged Isa. "Your mother said you were arriving today. Your young man is a blond! And a treat for the eyes, I must say."

"This is Richard," Isa said. "He speaks some Spanish."

Amanda flushed. "In a closed mouth flies don't enter."

"*Como?*" Richard said. "*Mucho gusto.*"

"Yes, indeed! Pleased to meet you."

"Cool elevator," Richard said. "Looks antique."

"What did he say?" Amanda asked.

"He admires the elevator," Isa said.

"You don't have one in America?"

"No."

"You must be glad to be home, then."

* * *

"You've cut your hair, Isabel," her mother said, stepping back from their embrace. "It suits you."

"About three years ago," Isa said. Her mother's hair had undergone that middle-aged Buenos Aires alchemy from brown to gold. "Is Juan still doing your hair?"

"It's gotten so light," her mother said, touching it. "The sun, you know."

"Do you like my hair?" Richard said in Spanish.

Isa's mother laughed and held out her hand. "You must be Richard. Your Spanish is excellent."

"It's very basic," Richard said. "*Mucho gusto, señora.*"

"I am also Isabel," her mother said. "You must call me that."

Isa's father appeared behind her mother in the doorway. His paunch had grown so that he tented over to kiss Isa, like a pregnant woman. He shook Richard's hand almost violently. "Mauricio. Very good to meet you, sir."

"Wow—a British accent," Richard said.

"A bit rusty, I'm afraid," her father said. "Do come in."

The front sitting room was jammed with furniture. The door to the dining room and the east wing of the apartment was shut, and from behind it came the sound of hammering and sawing.

"We are reforming," her father said.

"Renovating," Isa corrected him.

"I thought we'd put Richard in Hector's room," her mother said. Isa was surprised the maid's room off the kitchen was still called 'Hector's room.' Hector was her

139

mother's orphaned nephew, who'd come from Rosario to attend the University of Buenos Aires. He'd brought shaggy hair, a beard, rock music, and socialist opinions into their orderly household, and after a few months her father had asked him to move out.

"Isa has told me about Hector," Richard said.

"Like Isabel, he went abroad to study," Isa's father said.

"Have you heard from him?" Isa said.

"Hector never was good about staying in touch," Isa's mother said. She emitted a tiny sigh. "Isabel, on the other hand, wrote to us faithfully. You're going to sleep on the veranda off our bedroom," she added. "I've set up the cot."

Isa exchanged an amused glance with Richard—as she'd predicted, her parents would ensure that everyone stayed in his or her assigned bed. "Are my and Mayte's bedrooms being renovated also?" she asked.

"Everything on that side," her father said, gazing sternly at the door, as if that side of the house were being punished.

Isa's mother went into the kitchen and came back carrying a tray with coffee, hot milk, rolls and jam.

"Can I help?" Isa said.

"No, it's all done. Please, sit."

The dining table was pushed against the wall and the chairs were lined up facing a large gold-framed mirror. The four of them sat in a row as if at a lunch counter. Isa's hair was flat and greasy. Now that she followed American custom and washed and blow-dried it every day, it looked terrible when she didn't.

"How long has the work been going on?" she asked.

"Too long," her father said. "Reforms take forever in Argentina because workmen are lazy and incompetent. Nevertheless, some people believe the solution is to give the workers more power and more rights." As he said this he stared at Isa's reflection.

"Renovations take a long time in the States, too," Richard said.

"Then you realize what I am talking about. Men understand economics, eh?" He nudged Richard, who was sitting next to him.

"I have to go to the bathroom," Isa said. She stood up and squeezed past the other chairs and headed down the hall.

"Dry your hands on the blue towel," her mother called after her. "Our older daughter, Maria Teresa, will be here soon," she heard her mother telling Richard. "Isabel has never met her little niece and nephew."

Richard already knew that. He and Isa had been together since the morning she arrived at her freshman dorm, dazed and jetlagged. He asked her to go for coffee with him—before the six other guys on their floor who wanted to got the chance, he said later. As they walked along a snowy street in St. Paul, a woman rushed up to Isa, shouting that she was a murderer. Isa gasped and shrank back. She didn't realize the woman was talking about her mink coat. She thought, somehow, that she knew about Hector, that his disappearance was indeed Isa's fault.

Richard took charge of the situation, telling the woman

to get lost and ushering Isa into a nearby coffee shop as if she were a besieged starlet. Her English was pretty poor then, but over that day and late into that night she attempted to explain herself: her Barrio Norte childhood of convent schools and the tennis club and tea at five and Sunday drives in the Renault. About how Hector had blown into the apartment on Calle Austria like a hurricane. How he'd been arrested after a student demonstration and never seen again. How the police had assured her father that he'd gone into exile.

It was dawn when she fell asleep in Richard's dorm room; they both slept in and missed the first day of winter term. And later, when he seemed jealous about someone or other, she'd laugh and say, "I don't think he has time to hear the whole story."

In the bathroom, her mother's pots of face cream and her father's ivory-handled shaving brush were in their usual places on a shelf. They'd used these same items for as long as Isa could remember, and the sight of them moved her in a way that seeing her actual parents hadn't. She stared at her pale face in the mirror and burst into tears. Finally she splashed cold water on her eyes and dried her face on her mother's bathrobe.

Richard was waiting outside the bathroom door. "Did you fall in?"

"Kind of. Are Papa's opinions having a laxative effect on you, too?"

"He's just trying to bond over math skills, Isa."

"I can't stand it, and we've only been here half an hour."

"I think they're feeling shy, and don't know what to say to you."

"How about, 'How was college?' or 'Congratulations on your engagement?'"

"Chin up, your sister's here. She is pretty, though not as pretty as you."

"Now I'll never believe another word you say."

Because Mayte was beautiful—maybe even more now as an exhausted mother, with her hair loose and dark circles under her eyes, than with full makeup, in her glamorous power suits. She was a presenter on the evening news.

"My poor baby, with your red eyes—were you awake all night on the plane?" Mayte exclaimed, as if she and Isa had been separated for a brief vacation. Isa breathed in her warm, sweet, garlicky smell. Since she was little, she'd felt a powerful attraction to her sister that was almost, though not exactly, sexual. "Your boyfriend's cute," Mayte said. "Those blond eyebrows—so you know he doesn't dye his hair. And here are my little monsters—Adela, Eduardo, say hello to your Aunt Isa."

Isa had thought maybe she'd just gotten bad pictures of the kids, but they were both quite plain, almost simian, as if Mayte's and her husband Luis' good looks had cancelled each other out. Isa often felt nervous around small children, as around animals that might bite. She heard herself chattering at them in a high, perky voice—admiring the bunny embroidered on Adela's cardigan and the plastic car in Eduardo's fist—anything her eyes fell upon.

"I've brought you a present!" She rummaged through her backpack. "It's a video in English—your mama says you're already learning it. It's about a dog who solves crimes."

"Is it suitable for children, though?" her mother said.

"Not crimes, really. He revisits historical events to find out what really happened."

"Oh, dear."

"I hate for them to watch too much television," Mayte said.

"Is that a new policy?" her father asked dryly.

"Papa, you have absolutely no idea what my life is like," Mayte cried.

This had always been Mayte's core conviction: that nobody, nobody, could understand the complications, the difficulties, the demands of being Maria Teresa Conde. At the same time, her indignation covered everyone she loved like a righteous tidal wave: once she'd scolded a kid who put gum in Isa's hair until he wept. During the dictatorship she'd skirted the wrath of military authorities by focusing on mailorder scams, animal cruelty, stores that sold expired products. After the generals fell, she'd been one of the first to call for elections.

As if to prove that their mother's existence was untenable, Adela and Eduardo were clamoring loudly to put in the dog video. Isa expected her father to growl for silence, but he sighed and opened the newspaper.

"You won't enjoy it—it's in English," Mayte told them.

"I hate that shitty language," Adela wailed. "I can't understand it."

Janis

"*Yo también,*" said Richard, coming into the room.

"Could you tell us what the dog is saying?" Adela asked him.

"*Naturalmente,*" Richard said. Adela beamed at him and stuck her tongue out at her mother.

"Actually, we have to go," Mayte said.

"You're not staying for lunch?" Isa's mother said. "I've made *puchero.*"

"Impossible. I have to be dressed and at the studio in two hours. The four of you can eat it."

"But then there will be leftovers, and your father doesn't like to repeat."

"We could have it for supper," Isa said.

"We can't eat it after nine o'clock," her mother said reprovingly. "That's why Americans are so fat—they eat meat at night."

"Why don't you save the *puchero* for Saturday?" Mayte said. "The flavor will be better, and Luis can help eat it up."

"What will we do for lunch today, though?"

"Steak would be delicious," Isa said. "Argentina is famous for them."

Her mother looked at her and then at Richard. She prided herself on being a prudent household manager, but she was terribly cheap—their live-in maids never stayed long because she wouldn't raise their salaries. Isa knew that her mother would not want to spend money on steak for the four of them.

"Richard and I could go out to lunch," Isa said, after a long pause.

"That sounds like fun." Her mother looked relieved. "Papa and I could share a small steak—the butcher might have one left."

Mayte asked Isa to help her load the children into the car. Isa knew it was a pretext for a private conversation, and she looked forward to cozily trading complaints about their parents, like in the old days. "Mama sure hasn't changed," she said, as the elevator creaked and groaned its way to the ground floor. "She won't spring for steak, even for a homecoming lunch."

"You shouldn't have put her on the spot like that, Isa."

"It serves her right for being such a miser," Isa said. "And did you notice she kept averting her eyes from my ring? Like she'd never seen anything so vulgar."

It occurred to her that Mayte hadn't mentioned the ring, either.

"I think she and Papa are waiting for Richard to ask their permission to marry you," Mayte said.

"Permission? After I've been on my own for six years?"

Adela and Eduardo pushed the door open and ran up and down the hallway, their voices ringing against the tiles. It was good that they were the same age and could play together, Isa thought. Mayte was eight years older; another mother, really.

"When you took the bus from the airport this morning, did you wonder why Papa sold the Renault?" Mayte said. "He did it to pay for your college in America. He hardly got any engineering contracts after the fuss he made when Hector disappeared. Papa could have been arrested for that."

"Why would *Papa* be arrested if *Hector* left the country?"

"Because during the dictatorship it wasn't wise to ask too many questions. I'm not saying that was right," Mayte added quickly.

"What are you saying?"

"I'm saying Hector *could* have traveled somewhere very remote. Since the elections, exiles are coming back from all over the world—Nepal, Sweden. We're doing a segment about it, in fact."

"When he comes back he can have my room," Isa said. "I'm not staying."

"He can't have your room, because Mama and Papa are dividing the apartment into two and selling half," Mayte said. "They had no savings left by the time you graduated."

They were outside now, and Isa shivered in the thin autumn sunshine. The brown leaves of the sycamores rattled in the wind from the river. "It's not my fault," she said finally. "There was hyperinflation and everybody lost money. The generals were fucking the whole country, but Papa refused to believe it."

"Don't yell, please, Isabel," Mayte said.

"I'm not yelling." But she glanced around—into the windshields of cars along the curb and at the overgrown shrubs in the park across the street. "Besides, I can say what I like. It's a democracy now."

Mayte unlocked the passenger door and pulled down the front seat so that the children could climb into the back. Isa was shocked that they had no carseats.

"Fucking the whole country," Adela chanted. Eduardo giggled and joined in.

"Thanks for your help with the kids," Mayte said.

Upstairs, her parents and Richard were still sitting at the dining table, conversing with each other's reflections. "Richard has been telling us all about fishing with artificial flies," her mother said. "Americans are so practical to invent a way to avoid touching real flies."

"*La pesca a mosca* is popular in Patagonia," her father said. "On your next visit, you must bring your equipment and go there."

"You've made a good impression if Papa is already speaking of your next visit," Isa told Richard, as they strolled down Avenida Libertador. The cars zooming around the bronze Liberator monument looked tiny but fierce, like stinging bugs. "Even if he urged you to spend it in Patagonia."

He laughed. "I think your parents are glad to see you," he said.

"No, they're glad to see you. It's obvious they like you."

"Well, my parents like you."

"OK." Richard's family lived on an organic dairy farm, in the kind of harmony Isa had read indigenous peoples enjoyed before the arrival of the white man.

"Isabel and Mauricio told me they're worried about how you'll react to the news that they're downsizing and breaking up the apartment," he said.

Isabel and Mauricio? Isa scowled.

"They thought you'd be upset about losing your childhood bedroom, and they asked Mayte to tell you." He glanced at her uneasily. "But I guess she didn't get around to it."

"So you're telling me."

"I didn't want to know something you don't know, Isa. I believe it's better to be upfront and honest."

"I'll thank you not to call my family secretive and dishonest."

"Well, I agree it's weird they haven't said anything about our engagement."

"They want you to ask for my hand in marriage."

He whistled, shaking his head slowly. "After all those years of not even bothering to visit you?"

"They didn't have the money."

"Or didn't want to spend it—that's what you always said."

"So you won't ask them?"

"I don't see why I should. It makes no sense." Richard's face was set in a stubbornness she recognized, though never before directed at her. Maybe it had to do with suddenly being a foreigner. See how he liked it.

"Do things have to make sense?" she said.

"In my view, yes."

"That is stupid and closed-minded."

Passers-by were slowing their steps discreetly to observe them—it was not yet usual in Argentina for a couple of *yanqui* tourists to be arguing in the middle of the sidewalk on Avenida Libertador. "It makes it less tempting to storm off in a huff," Richard said at last, smiling, "when you've got all the pesos in your purse."

"Dollars are welcome everywhere. So feel free to get out of my sight."

His smile faded. He turned and boarded a bus that was paused at the curb; the doors slammed and it pulled away.

Isa ran after the bus as it chuffed on down the street. She guessed Richard would get off at the next stop—a bus driver wouldn't actually want to deal with American coins.

The doors slid open, but he didn't appear. She watched him making his way to the rear of the bus, his yellow head bobbing above the others in the aisle. Perhaps the driver had taken pity and waved him on; perhaps the attractive woman walking behind him, having observed him respond so patiently to his harridan girlfriend, had paid his fare. She would sit down in the seat next to him, and when he thanked her, she would ask where he was from. She would tell him she was studying English. They would laugh and flirt and fall in love.

Isa stood at the crosswalk and tried to decide what to do. Richard's bus was headed to the Plaza San Martin. Most likely he'd get off there and catch another bus back uptown. They'd spot each other more easily if she was on foot on the other side of the avenue.

She crossed Libertador and headed south along the river. It was cold, and the only other people on the promenade were old men in black berets, exiles from the Spanish Civil War, killing time before lunch. The Spanish dictator had been dead ten years, and yet here they remained, playing chess on the stone benches and arguing in Galician. Ahead of her loomed equestrian statues to the heroes of independence and Indian extermination, shrouded in a pinkish mist Isa used to recall on stark Minnesota winter days. It was not— she now realized—the gauze of memory but exhaust from unleaded gasoline.

She circled the Plaza San Martin, under the giant rubber trees. Richard was not in the bus queues. Perhaps his pretty seatmate had gotten off with him, and, still chatting, they'd decided to stroll down the pedestrian walkway at Calle Florida. So Isa went that way, plunging into the marmalade-thick crowd of lunchtimes shoppers.

She passed the storefront language school where she'd once taken classes. English had seemed to her a simple language back then, with its unadorned verbs and genderless nouns. Maybe the pretty seatmate still thought that. And maybe, having a bit of time before class, she'd suggest to Richard that they keep walking, even though they'd have exhausted their conversational abilities and not be saying much, just acknowledging their growing attraction by occasionally brushing against each other on purpose. Finally the seatmate might venture, "Do you have a thirst? Because a famous cafe of leftist intellectuals is here, in front."

"Cafe La Paz," Richard would read, holding the door for her. *"Eso suena familar."*

Isa went inside the cafe. It was nearly empty, and quiet but for the murmur of the TV over the bar. She sat at a small table in the corner, opposite the large round one where Hector used to hold court, surrounded by his *compañeros.* They didn't discuss politics in public—at least not so Isa understood—although there were a lot of jokes and slang that made people suddenly laugh, or grow thoughtful. Isa would scoot her chair up next to him, the worshipful younger cousin with her satchel of grammar workbooks.

Now, Isa recognized the waiter approaching her, though he was grayer, his mustache droopier, like a plant needing water. Clearly he didn't recognize her, with her short hair and American clothes.

She ordered a beer. The waiter bowed, then hesitated. "Something else, miss?"

"There used to be so many students here."

"In the seventies, yes. Then later, not so many." He made no move to go get her drink.

"And a cheese sandwich," Isa said.

He bowed again, but stood as if glued to a spot on the floor. Was he quite right in the head? "There was a handsome guy with dark curls who used to sit at that table," she said. "Hector Rodriguez. I wonder what became of him."

"We heard that the students went abroad to study."

"Actually, I did."

"So it was true, then. I thought you looked foreign, although you speak normally." He tucked his tray under his arm and walked away.

Overhead, Mayte was reading the afternoon news. Compared to American reporters, her expression was severe, even grim. There was a clip showing a family at the airport, rushing to embrace someone disembarking. Then a shot of an empty courtroom, a judge in robes walking up steps, footage of the generals on the balcony of the presidential palace. Isa had read that the junta was to be put on trial, but the sound was too low for her to hear what Mayte was saying about it.

When the waiter returned with her beer and sandwich she said, pointing to the TV, "Those sons of bitches will go to jail."

He shrugged. "They'll say, 'Prove there are *desaparecidos.*' And nobody can. Because they have disappeared."

The last time Isa saw Hector was after the window got broken at the Banco Espiritu Santo. She'd come across the demonstration by accident, and gotten off the bus to watch. Police arrived quickly; the students scattered, but nobody paid any attention to Isa on the sidewalk across the street in her plaid uniform.

This had given her an idea.

The next afternoon, at the cafe, she'd whispered to Hector that she had something important to tell him, and waited until all the others had gone back to class.

"O.K., Cousin, what's your big news?" Hector drummed his fingers on the table to the music that seemed always to be playing in his head. Since Isa's father had asked him to leave the apartment, that's what he called her—Cousin. He was making it clear what they were to each other, the distance that had to be between them.

She was ready to join the cause, she told him.

Hector's hands went still. "What cause?"

"I can carry messages. I look like a schoolgirl. Nobody will suspect."

"You are a schoolgirl. And you're mistaken, Cousin—there's nothing to join."

"But I believe in the things you believe in."

"Well, I believe I'm about to miss my physics exam." He stood up, clapping his hands on his pockets. "And I don't even have a pencil. Could you loan me one, pretty please?"

Slowly, with a superior smile, Isa took two pencils from her pencil box and handed them to him.

"Sharpened! I promise I'll return them." He kissed her on both cheeks. "*Ciao.*" Outside in the bus queue, he turned and waved, then pushed his way aboard: the bus was crowded and he was late.

He was nineteen, the cousin she was so in love with that she used to sit cross-legged on his bed in the maid's room, thumbing through his textbooks and listening to his records, waiting into the early morning for him to come home. Nineteen when he boarded a bus and was never seen again.

"Isabel is too young," her father had said to Hector, a year earlier, as Isa lingered in the hallway, listening. "She cannot master her emotions."

"It's cool." Hector had used the English expression. He was packing his suitcases. "I was sixteen once, myself, Uncle."

"Good, then," her father had said. "As men, we understand each other."

Then they'd carried his bags to the elevator and her father had driven Hector to the student dormitory where he'd live for the last year of his life.

Isa was certain of this, as she sat alone in the cafe with her untouched food in front of her. She could picture Richard falling for an Argentinean stranger, but she couldn't imagine her cousin traveling the world incommunicado. He was too noisy; too vivid. Alive, Hector would have found some way to get in touch.

She left money on the table and hurried out of the cafe. It was late afternoon now, and the light was low, slanting and silvery. She walked back along rush-hour-choked streets toward Barrio Norte, past walls decoupaged with shredding campaign posters and dead-eyed student I.D. photos. The Xeroxed photographs all bore the same query beneath: Have You Seen? A cold drizzle began to fall. She was crying as she walked, and looked insane perhaps, so no men bothered her; no one made eye contact.

She would stay and attend the military trials. She'd move into Hector's room, get a job teaching English to contribute to the household. She'd persuade her mother to don a white scarf and march with the mothers of the disappeared. She'd give her evidence, meager and ridiculous as it was: *Hector Rodriguez borrowed two pencils from me and promised to return them.*

155

Richard would understand.

No, he wouldn't. But he'd go home and find someone who truly loved him. She slid her ring off her finger.

Her parents were at the dining table with the remains of tea in front of them, barricaded behind their heaped-up furniture. Even with her father's girth and her mother's gleaming hair, they looked smaller and older than they had just this morning. "Richard said you'd be back later," Isa's mother said. "He ate quite a number of sandwiches with his tea. Was your lunch all right?"

"Not really," Isa said.

"He asked us for your hand," her father said. "In Spanish, so it was hard to know what he was getting at, at first."

"He told us about the plan to live in a little log house in the woods," her mother said. "Do you remember how you loved that American storybook when you were small, Isabel? You made your sister read it to you over and over again. So I suppose all this was foretold." She sighed.

"But he's a fine fellow," her father said.

"He is," Isa said.

"What's happened to your ring?" her mother said.

"It's in my pocket." Isa took it out but didn't put it back on.

"Good idea. There's so much crime now that the generals have gone. Papa and I don't dare go out after sundown."

"Where is Richard?" Isa glanced around, as if he might be hiding somewhere in this crowded, crazy room.

She had to talk to him quickly, before she lost heart.

By the time she got down to the street the rain had cleared, and the traffic lights at Libertador gleamed unnaturally bright. Cement-colored clouds rushed across the sky toward Uruguay; the river shone like burnished steel. On the promenade, she saw Richard leaning against the parapet, talking to some fisherman with spinners and a bloody bucket of bait. He'd be practicing his new words: *Me gusta la pesca a mosca.*

Then he turned and saw her. He broke into a smile, waving. All was settled; all was forgiven. But she stood rooted, unable to move forward, while the lights changed, and then changed again.

Miguel Rivera

"You know the old man I was playing backgammon with on the beach?" Philip said to Lila, as they finished their dinner of grilled snapper on the patio of the Hotel Tropical. They were spending the week on an island in Mexico. "Guess where he's from." But he didn't wait for her to guess. "Uruguay," he said.

"Everyone's from Uruguay," Lila said. "It's like when you learn a new vocabulary word, and suddenly you hear it everywhere." The dizziness she'd felt earlier in the day, in the marketplace, returned. She slipped her foot out of her sandal and rubbed it on the top of Philip's foot. She could feel the raised scars he would have for the rest of his life.

"I asked him if he knew Miguel Rivera," Philip said. "Since Uruguay's a small place."

"I hope you didn't explain why you were asking," Lila said,

smiling. You never knew what Philip would come out with. "We met coming over on the hydrofoil," he'd say, when asked, as they frequently were, if he and Lila were honeymooners. Actually, they'd been married ten years. They were both thirty-seven, tall and slim, with wavy brown hair. When they were younger, people had sometimes assumed they were brother and sister, and it had amused Philip to pretend that they were.

"I said he did some work for us," Philip said, refilling both their wine glasses. "Which is true in a way. He got us to a beach in Mexico at the height of tax season, drinking piña coladas and reading and having sex in the middle of the day."

"Are you sorry we came?"

"I thank God for Miguel Rivera," Philip said, and his eyes glistened in the light of the flaming dessert the waiter had just brought to their table.

During their first few sessions with Ruth, the marriage counselor, Philip had referred to Miguel Rivera, reasonably enough, as "the son of a bitch." Then one day he'd said "the Uruguayan guy." A ghost of a smile had crossed his features as his eyes met Lila's. She'd giggled.

"Why are you laughing, Lila?" Ruth had asked.

"She's picturing Uruguay Guy," Philip had said. "In his tights."

"Are you, Lila?"

But Lila had only laughed harder.

After they'd left the counselor's office, Philip had resumed his gloomy, wounded air, as if Lila were increasing the poison dosage in his food. Then the next week, at Ruth's, he'd suddenly said, "Miguel Rivera," as if he'd been racking his brain for the name for weeks. Lila's cheeks went hot.

"How do you feel?" Ruth had asked her.

"Embarrassed,' Lila had said. "And sorry to have caused all this trouble."

"I have an idea, Lila," Philip had said, in a loud, conspiratorial whisper. "Let's flee to Mexico."

Lila had met the man called Miguel Rivera at her job teaching English as a Second Language at a community center in suburban Maryland. Her Beginning students seemed to have the hardest lives, and she jumped around a lot to keep them awake, in the evenings after their second jobs. The Intermediate students tended to complain about the nonsensical rules of English grammar, as if Lila were in a position to lobby for change. The Advanced classes were capable of real conversations, but they were also the most adept at cheating. One, a fur-coated Iranian, had turned in a touching essay about life in exile that had been lifted from Oprah's magazine, as Lila discovered months later in the dentist's office.

Miguel Rivera had dropped out after three Advanced lessons, too late for a refund, though he'd asked for one. He'd sat in the back, like a teenaged troublemaker, his leather jacket squeaking as he crossed his arms—a beetle-browed, heavyset Che Guevara.

"You are our first Uruguayan," Lila had said, then walked

over and stuck a new pushpin into her big, multicolored map of the world. His lip had curled slightly. Well, foreign language classes were unavoidably infantilizing; as in elementary school, they spent a lot of time on the iconography of American holidays: pumpkins, Pilgrims, turkeys, trees.

"I am from Colonia, not Montevideo," Miguel Rivera had said.

"All right, then!" Lila had replied gaily, and moved the pushpin. Again the mocking smile. His English was fine, but he'd only speak in class if called upon.

One dark winter's night, Lila told Philip that she'd had an affair with a Uruguayan student who'd dropped her class. It came out in the midst of an argument, the kind of argument they'd once declared they'd rather blow their brains out than have, about who did more around the house. As usual, Lila was winning. And what did she win? Philip's jaw clamped shut like a nutcracker's, as he perused her array of grievances, jumbled and bleak as items in a yard sale. Declaring her the victor, he'd spend even more time at the office, be even less engaged with her and the children—she could see it already, in those painted-wood eyes.

Maybe she'd get his attention if she confessed that she'd had an affair? Her question was joking, rhetorical. Philip's response was not. Suddenly, the wooden man came alive. "You're kidding, right?"

"What if I'm not?"

"Lila, you are kidding."

"No." She'd tell him the truth in a second. Meanwhile—he was actually looking into her face. It had taken thirteen words. But wasn't it only sixteen lying words that had led to a war?

"Who is he?"

Lila couldn't recall the name of the Che Guevara student. "Miguel Rivera," she said. It fit him. Saying it, she felt the protective fondness one feels for an old boyfriend. How strange—she hadn't realized she was attracted to him until just now.

"I'll kill the son of a bitch."

Lila froze, even though he was the kind of person who scooped up bees and spiders in a Tupperware and carried them outside. "Wait, Philip."

He spun around on a Matchbox car and fell down the stairs. Lila wanted to throw herself after him, but gripped the handrail for the sake of the children. They were out of bed, all three, screaming in their footed pajamas; there was blood everywhere.

"Who would have thought the old man had so much blood in him?" That was the first thing Philip said when he came to, still lying where he'd landed, and Lila wept for joy that he was not a vegetable. If he was paralyzed, she'd read to him; take dictation for his memoir; she'd refuse to assist his suicide.

He came out of surgery shortly after midnight. Delicate metal scaffolding encased his ankle, an engineering marvel whose actual cost was shielded from people like them, with excellent insurance. The blood had come out of Philip's head, which for some reason was not such a worrying place to bleed from. The bandage on his forehead was small. One of his eyes looked like it would be black tomorrow.

"The first thing we do is sue the pants off Matchbox," Philip said. "Easy for you to laugh, Lila. What's all over your clothes? You're like Jackie Kennedy—except, of course, not a blameless widow."

"No," Lila said, with a chortling sob. "We need to talk."

"Not while I'm drugged, please. I want to enjoy every minute. Why don't we go and see that Ruby person you're always raving about?"

"Ruth. I don't know that she's such a wonder, I've simply heard—"

"Hush, darling. Hold my hand. Put it—there. Good girl. Is that a nurse at the door? It's a porn movie come true—oh, Lila, you spoilsport."

It could be argued that Lila's lie had refreshed the marriage; revived Philip's antic spirit, which had seemingly been crushed by riding Metro every morning to Foggy Bottom; even given him quality time with the kids. His foot elevated on cushions, he held court in the living room within sight of the blood-stained wall, about which he wove wilder and wilder tales of an epic battle with alien attackers. "Noo, Daddy! That's not what happened!" they shrieked, delighted. To them Philip was a rock star in their own home, who made up funny songs about them on his old Fender. They didn't care if he didn't know the name of the pediatrician who'd treated them for seventeen years—they were seven, five and five. The afternoon before his fall, Philip had called Lila from work to get the man's particulars for a form—he didn't even know in which state the doctor's office was located—and she'd let her outrage simmer gently, covered, through dinner, baths, stories, bed.

In Mexico they walked hand in hand on the edge of the sand. They danced by the light of the moon. Philip still limped, but he'd been ordered to keep moving. "Car accident," he'd say, to strangers' enquiries. "It was a winter night, and I lost control of the vehicle. Luckily, my wife emerged without a scratch." He'd slip his hand around Lila's bare, tanned waist.

"People are a lot more inquisitive than they'd be at home," Lila said. "Is it because we're all foreigners together, or because we're all in bathing suits?"

"I heard we're going to be voted this week's Cutest Couple," Philip said, and laughed at the look on her face.

Lila supposed they did look cute, playing murderous games of backgammon in the shade of their palm-roofed *palapa*. They passed exotic cocktails and interesting *New Yorker* articles back and forth. She ran into the water and came out, dripping, and felt his hungry gaze, as if she were the one who'd almost died tripping over a toy.

She flung herself down in the hot sand. She'd vowed to come clean with Philip before the end of their vacation, and now there were only two days left.

Lila had expected the real story to come out in their sessions with Ruth; that a trained psychologist would instantly diagnose the lie by observing her posture, her voice, the way she fiddled with her purse strap or pushed back her hair. But Ruth, with her planed cheekbones and neutral pantsuits, accepted whatever you said at face value—the truth was apparently up to Lila, not her.

She stood, brushed herself off, and put on the fringed terry cloth garment the hotel provided to make female guests presentable to the villagers.

"I'm going into town to buy some mangoes, want to come?"

"No, I'll sit. My foot's been aching."

"Ouch." She gave herself a few strokes with an invisible scourge, then set out across the beach with her new plastic net shopping bag.

The road to the village was dusty and hot. The imperial palms that shaded their little corner of paradise were evidently not native to the island. A few years ago, a hurricane had blown away the colonial-era adobe village, and the place was now "spoilt," according to their British guidebook. Rebar poked optimistically out of cinderblock where second stories would go, if only enough trinkets could be sold to foreigners. Philip and Lila had done their part, buying up a carry-on-full of t-shirts, obsidian chess sets, and sharks' tooth necklaces, not only for the children but for Lila's parents, who were babysitting. Lila had hardly been able to face them, after having understood, in Ruth's sphinxlike presence, that they'd ruined what she'd thought was a perfectly happy childhood. Another revelation had been a sordid kiss between Philip and a fellow tax lawyer, some years ago, in an empty conference room.

"What did you conclude from that, Philip?" Ruth had asked.

"Never try to feel up a woman wearing a sports bra," Philip had said. "I was like one of those coyotes in a trap, ready to gnaw off my hand."

Even Ruth had cracked a smile. But if a person makes you even unhappier than you were before, what can you do except turn against her? Philip referred to Ruth as "the refrigerator," though she was quite petite. So they'd made a run for it, against the one piece of advice the shrink had voiced: they weren't done with therapy; it was the psychological equivalent of taking half a course of antibiotics. "So Lila's in danger of spreading adultery germs in Mexico," Philip had said. "Don't worry. I won't let her out of my sight."

Lila strolled through the tarp-covered marketplace, breathing in the smells of chocolate, peppers, and raw meat. She realized she hadn't been alone since they'd arrived. On the other hand, she was almost never alone. Every minute of her life was accounted for—how could Philip have believed she even had time for an affair? Miguel Rivera, indeed!

Then all at once she saw him, on the other side of a mountain range of dried *chipotles* and *piquillos*, studying a display of hand-tooled belts. He was wearing a tight black t-shirt; aviator sunglasses were pushed up on top of his large, leonine head. A leather rucksack was slung over one shoulder. Miguel Rivera looked up—straight at Lila, in her straw hat and big glasses and turquoise penitent's robe. She understood she was gawking when he lifted his hand in friendly, impersonal greeting, as a besieged movie star might. She turned and fled the market, toward the quay, where fresh tourists were pouring out of the hydrofoil.

She darted along the seawall until she reached the beach, then jogged across the sand to the water's edge before slowing to a walk, panting. Surely—it couldn't have been Miguel Rivera. The man must be a common national physical type— perhaps a Uruguayan type—a phenomenon she and Philip had observed years earlier, backpacking through Europe. Or maybe she'd hallucinated. A light breakfast, a killer Margarita, a walk under the blistering sun, the shadowy market with its overpowering odors.

She put her hat and sunglasses and cover-up on top of the shopping bag and waded into the cool water. She dived under a small wave. The current here, at the tip of the island, was much stronger than it was down by the hotel. It was carrying her, as if she were a football, out to sea. She tried to swim back, but the current wouldn't let her. It gripped her tightly, swaddling her. Of course—there was nobody around. Of course—she was going to drown. How ridiculous.

Though this was a good thing to know, at the end: she was more tranquil in the face of her own death than she'd been in the face of Philip's. She wasn't as cowardly as she'd thought—she'd go back to Ruth and tell her so. To Ruth, Lila had talked a lot about her fears—of horses, of brain tumors, of the children riding bikes to school. Though not, obviously, of her fear of telling Philip the truth—that the marital spark she'd ignited would be extinguished. Oh, right: she wouldn't be seeing Ruth, or anyone else, again. But now the current had decided to carry her calm, resigned body in an arc back toward the beach.

She staggered up onto the sand. Her shopping bag was nowhere in sight, but the waving palms of the hotel were less than fifty yards away. She walked up to their *palapa*, where Philip was still sitting in its feathery afternoon shadow. He was playing backgammon with a handsome white-haired man of about sixty—an age, they'd recently agreed, that no longer seemed elderly. Philip looked up and smiled and drew her to him. "So you swam back from the market?"

"Without exactly meaning to. There's a wicked rip tide."

"My wife, Lila, used to be a champion swimmer," Philip said. "She's from California."

"Ah, California," the white-haired man said dreamily, as her students often did. It was a place everyone in the world had heard of. "Is San Francisco as beautiful as they say?" He had a faint, unplaceable accent.

"It is," Lila said. "Well, I'm going back to the room to take a shower."

"I'll be up in a minute," Philip said. "As soon as I finish off this unsuspecting gentleman."

"That's where you're wrong, sir—that's where you're wrong."

Unlike Lila, who didn't speak to strangers unless she had to, Philip made friends wherever he went. Such charm had its downside—at Ruth's they'd discovered that they'd both always supposed they might one day consult a marriage counselor because of his bad behavior, rather than hers. But he was an equal-opportunity flirt, melting musty-breathed old aunts, sullen teenagers. Lila. They'd been introduced a couple of years out of college; his Don Juan reputation had preceded him. "So I guess I'm Miss February," she'd said once, early on.

"No, I don't think so," he'd said, suddenly solemn. "I really don't think so."

Lila showered and then crawled between the marvelously crisp, smooth hotel sheets that could never be duplicated at home, no matter what you spent on thread count. When she woke, the light in the room was almost gone, and Philip was whispering in her ear.

"What? I was dreaming."

"I said where are the mangoes you went to buy? I'm afraid we're going to have to frisk you, Ma'am."

So she was living a lie—was that really the worst thing? Any reader of newspaper advice columns could tell you it was. But it was a condition she was coping with, and, like any serious condition, it had heightened her awareness, her sensations, her gratitude.

* * *

170

They finished their flaming dessert and ordered espressos. At home, Lila couldn't even drink decaf at night. Philip poured cream with abandon—there was no cholesterol on a tropical island, either. "Speaking of the Uruguayan—I'll be damned," he said, dropping his spoon. "Don't look now, Lila. Listen: this afternoon, while we're playing backgammon, the old guy tells me he's meeting a former flame here at the hotel, a singer who's been trying to break out, in the States. So I picture—I don't know—a cross between Carmen Miranda and Renee Fleming. Now, turn your head a little— casual-like, to the left."

Out of the corner of her eye Lila saw the white-haired Uruguayan cross the patio, heading toward the hotel bar. On his arm was Miguel Rivera. Never having seen Lila's supposed lover, Philip, of course, didn't recognize him.

"Somehow I never think of old people being gay," Philip said.

"One mustn't make assumptions," Lila finally managed to say.

"Can't tell a book by its cover."

"Sauce for the goose."

They were laughing now, a little wildly. Then their eyes locked. "Whatever I did that drove you to it, Lila, I'm sorry."

"No, I'm sorry." She began to cry. He reached for her hand.

"Why don't we take a walk on the beach?" he said sooth- ingly, as if she were five and wailing. "We might even find your bag. Weren't those sunglasses prescription?"

"Anyone who tries to wear them is in for a shock," Lila said. "The world through my eyes is not pretty. But how's your foot?"

"Feelin' stronger every day," Philip sang.

She went back to their room for her Mexican cotton shawl. Walking along the breezeway, she crossed paths with the man-who-couldn't-possibly-be-Miguel-Rivera. "Mrs. Murphy?"

She stopped. He leaned toward her. She could smell woodsy cologne and tequila. "Are you—?"

"I am Eduardo Romero, from Advanced English class. But I dropped it. Dropped out, I think you say."

Lila felt the blood rush to her face. "I thought it might be you, in the market this afternoon. But I decided the coincidence was too great."

"You were the lady in blue, near the hydrofoil landing? I must apologize."

"There's no need!" she cried.

"I told the school director you were a bad, boring teacher. In reality, my life was not going well. But suddenly, here in Mexico, everything is better. My friend says he might move to America to be with me."

"Is he also Uruguayan?"

"How amazing that you remember where I come from! I confess I worried later that you might lose your job because of my complaint."

She shook her head. "I've been there for years. They de-

cided you were one disgruntled customer out of many satis-
fied ones."

"I'm going to write to the school and tell them you're a
good teacher!" He was pretty drunk, Lila realized.

"That's kind of you." He'll never write, she thought, as she
walked away. But, like most people, he had admirable inten-
tions.

"What were you doing all that time?" Philip said plaintively, when she got back to the table. He'd been making little
dunes with spilled sugar.

"Having sex with a stranger."

"Figures."

He sighed and leaned on her arm, like an old man. Ahead
of them, the moon shimmered on the dark water. Lila was
not in it, floating, a corpse waiting until daybreak to be
found. "Tell me every lurid, prurient detail. Leave nothing
out."

"Okay," Lila said. She took a deep breath.

Looker

Norah Larson's beauty came to the Minnesota prairie with her ancestors: an impractical treasure, like a hand-painted vase or a chiming clock wrapped in quilts. "Pretty is as pretty does," her Swedish grandmother said, sternly.

"You mother's a looker, all right," Norah's father would say, gazing at his beautiful wife descending the stairs dressed for a church supper, a dental school reunion. Norah's mother would smile, in a way that Norah at thirteen supposed had to do with sex and later realized expressed a profounder satisfaction: that of having made, out of a crowd of suitors, the right choice.

But Norah experienced the peak of her own golden looks as a kind of hurricane, one that carried her to San Sebastian with the writer who'd spoken at her college graduation and was headed there on a fellowship, then to Madrid with a married Socialist politician so publicly esteemed that for years she disbelieved her private reality, and finally to Barcelona with a painter who—refreshingly, she'd thought at the time—never pretended to be anything but a pill.

When she left him and returned to Madrid she was forty-two, and felt that she was home again, though she'd never set out to become a Spaniard. For twenty years, she'd held Spain at arm's length, believing only love was keeping her there, and she was surprised by how the sight of the overbearing palaces and sooty monuments of the capital moved her, as if she'd spent her childhood playing in its dusty, treeless plazas.

"You were Spanish in another life," declared her friend, Eva, who was a professional fortune-teller. Eva's clientele had grown during Norah's absence from Madrid so that she now kept a suite at the Hotel Reina Victoria where she received celebrities: actors, soccer players, TV journalists. But she'd cancelled her next hour's appointments and ordered tea from room service when Norah showed up. She hadn't foreseen this visit—she admitted that.

"In my past life I was a babe," Norah said, as the two of them lolled like schoolgirls on the brocaded sofas of the suite's sitting room. "It's a relief to be plump and middle-aged and fade quietly into the woodwork."

"Bollocks," said Eva, who was British, though she didn't look it, with her long, black hair and floaty, gypsylike clothes. Her Spanish was rudimentary still; judging from the way she'd ordered the tea, though this probably only deepened her clients' impression that she was channeling messages from another world.

Now she bent over the cards she'd laid out on the table, like a doctor reviewing an x-ray. "Look here, Norah—your knave of hearts is a musician, clearly. The second queen so close by? That's a triangle."

"Maybe I'll meet a musician who plays the triangle," Norah said. Eva smiled, but she folded the cards away quickly into a silk scarf, as though joking might damage them.

There'd been a time when Norah had hung on every word of Eva's predictions. She'd read the books her friend had pressed onto her, about Uri Gellar, ESP, mysteriously patterned roads in the highlands of Peru. But she no longer believed there was a future laid out for mortals to read. She wondered if Eva did, deep down. They'd both been *profesoras de inglés* at a language school during the wild eighties after Franco's death. Eva had read cards then, too—as a means of keeping everybody awake between three and four in the morning.

Now she was settled down with Juan, her off-and-on lover of many years. He was an old man, an *intelectual público*, whom Norah still occasionally glimpsed on Spanish talk shows.

"You must come round for a meal," Eva said. "We're fixing up Juan's flat—it's a huge, drafty old place on Arenal. But it had no bathtub, if you please, and a kitchen with one gas ring."

Norah had once spent a weekend at Juan's place; a fact, it appeared, that Eva still did not know. "Then the rumors are true—you cook now?" Norah said, in a loud, bright voice, as if this was what she'd returned to Madrid to verify.

"One could, if one took the bubble wrap off the cooker," Eva said. "Juan will be glad to hear you're among us again, Norah. He's always been fond of you."

There was nothing meaning in her look or tone that Norah could detect. Evidently Juan had kept his promise not to tell Eva about their affair, if you could even call it that. It had happened just before Norah left for Barcelona with the painter. Juan and Eva had split up, seemingly for good. Who'd have predicted that they'd reconcile? Not Eva. She'd flown to London; later Juan followed and wooed her back. And Norah was gone by then—she was gone from Madrid for ten years.

Eva went to the ornate desk in the corner and took out a sheet of hotel stationery and a gold pencil. She seemed comfortable in her elegant new surroundings—well, they were new to Norah. "Here's my mobile number. You've got one now, haven't you?"

"I hate them," Norah said, so emphatically that Eva laughed.

"Quite the prisoner's anklet, aren't they? Never mind, Norah; ring when you're settled in a flat."

"You bet," Norah said.

But she put off calling, even after she'd found an apartment, which turned out to be kitty-corner to the Reina Victoria. Norah's balcony faced her favorite plaza, the Plaza Santa Ana, where she was pleased to see that elderly men in black berets still convened on benches in the sun, like extras in a long-running musical.

She didn't believe in reincarnation any more, but she did feel, coming back to Madrid, that she'd been given a chance to start over. This time around, she knew which street markets had the best produce; at which café she wanted to become a regular. She made an appointment at her old language school for an interview.

"Norah Larson—you're quite famous," the new director said. He was American, and wore a square of beard under his lower lip like a carpet sample.

"What am I famous for?" Norah said, to which he only smiled—smirked. She stood to go, but not before naming an astronomical salary, to teach him a lesson.

"No problem. Can you start next week?"

So she took the job—for now. Living provisionally had turned out to be what she was good at. Part of her clung to the notion that she might "go home" at any moment—though the Minnesota friends she still exchanged Christmas cards with were absorbed in acronyms alien to her: PTA, AYSO, ADHD. Wasn't it better, she always ended up concluding, to be a real foreigner rather than just feel like one? And her parents, retired now, had come to rely on their winter pilgrimage to visit her. They often declared they loved Spain, as though Norah's delightful, romantic surroundings were a son-in-law.

Such an interesting, dynamic young man, they'd said, of

this Spanish beau or that one, though when they heard of the demise of a love affair they commended Norah for being choosy. But love, for her, was a storm that passed and left her blinking, baffled, at a cloudless sky. Out of the wreckage she'd salvaged a couple of handsome nude portraits of herself, and a dedicated copy of the novelist's latest book, though she thought the heedless young heroine recalled his demented rants about her, rather than the truth. She'd once been told that she'd helped inspire Spain's divorce law, though after its passage her Socialist lover had found other impediments to marrying her.

Yes, she was a *solterona*, a spinster. She began saying this as a joke, though the idea was oddly pleasing, as were the rituals of solo housekeeping, which recalled her solitary play as a child. She filled her new apartment with plants, which the painter had loathed. With her princely salary, she bought a teacher's wardrobe of tweed skirts and cashmere cardigans; her style, she concluded wryly, was that of an ex-nun with a trust fund.

Nuns were a vanishing breed in Spain, and other types of single women were still exotic. At the language school, Norah's twentysomething students found it hard to fathom a woman nearly the age of their mothers who had only to answer to herself. Honestly—she didn't cook Sunday lunch for anyone?

"Only for my class, so please come," she said impulsively, and panicked when everyone accepted. She stayed up half the night baking trays of lasagna which they nibbled at—

Spaniards are suspicious of foreign recipes. What they approved of was her cool, funky apartment: the racy pen-and-ink drawings of her, the photos and books and *objets*, all the loot of past love. She told herself that it wasn't hard to impress the impressionable, but she couldn't help liking the picture reflected in her students' eyes: of the worldly ex-courtesan, who'd enjoyed life and hadn't let it shipwreck her. Soon Norah's Sunday afternoon salon was a regular event, fueled by proper Spanish *tapas*—pickled mussels, sardines, cold squares of omelet—ordered from the bar across the plaza.

It was at one of these gatherings that she met Rafael Balboa. Norah didn't know who he was. Like many guests in her new circle, he showed up with a guitar, but when he began to play the whole room went quiet: he had a soft voice until it flamed out into a flamenco wildness and then banked back again, sweet and jazzy.

"You're talented," Norah said at last. "You ought to perform in public." The silence around her told her of her mistake.

He nodded without looking at her. He was possibly thirty, with the antique handsomeness of a Roman coin. Mortified, she went out to the balcony on the pretext of collecting wine glasses, and he followed. "If you liked my music, I'll send you my CD," he said.

Norah blushed and shook her head. She wished he'd take his guitar and leave, letting this embarrassment be a cautionary tale. But Rafa planted himself on a balcony chair and poured wine into two of the used glasses. What could she do but trot out her best charm and flattery—all those tricks she'd thought she'd better learn to despise before they became pathetic?

They stayed talking on the balcony after the other guests left, into the morning, then went to bed. Well, why not? He loved her, she loved him—you could announce this fearlessly in Spanish, because *te quiero* also means "I want you." They lay nose to nose; panting; then dozed finally. They woke, mid-afternoon, the Venetian blinds painting their bodies with buttery stripes, ready to pounce again. The five o'clock bells were chiming in the plaza when Rafa jumped out of bed and into his clothes, muttering about being late for a rehearsal.

Maybe he was. But it was fine if he'd made that up; she might be reckless still, but she was no longer foolish. Holding her chenille robe closed at the throat, she walked him to the door. They bowed and thanked each other, with playful ceremony—hostess and guest—and said farewell.

An hour later, he buzzed the street intercom. Norah glanced around her disheveled apartment. She'd forgotten this particular one-night stand awkwardness: leaving a possession you couldn't live without at the scene. One more reason to have this event be the last of its kind, she thought, as she pulled open her heavy wooden door.

"I've taken your advice about performing in public," Rafa said, panting now from running upstairs. He held out a complimentary ticket to a nightclub in a suburb that was, in Norah's urban mind, halfway to Portugal.

Getting there involved switching metro lines three times until the train reached a dreary outlying station: a cluster of fascist-era highrises on a windswept plateau. Suburbia had never really caught on, in Spain. So he wasn't that famous— not yet. Inside, the club was a particularly bleak combination of derelict and new. And the audience was all wrong for Rafa's music: mere teenagers, in ugly getups that clinked like armor. Regarding Norah, as some did, they might have supposed that the lady with the big, middleaged purse was Rafael Balboa's music instructor. She'd been a teacher long enough to recognize children in costume, and when she turned around, glowering, and shushed them, they more or less did.

Rafa insisted on driving her home. "What a wretched dive!" Norah said, as they sped back to the city in a tiny green car.

"Yes, but it belongs to my cousin, so I wanted to help him out," Rafa said. "The car's his, too. I have to get it back early tomorrow morning." He glanced over at her. "Would you rather I didn't stay over?"

"I'd rather prove to you that not everything I say is grotesquely tactless."

If everyone has a defect they're secretly proud of, tactlessness was Norah's. She had a good eye and ear—the novelist had realized this, long ago, which was probably the reason he'd brought her along to San Sebastian, like a dictionary. She could be presented with anything—a painting, a political speech, a song—and say where it was right and where it wasn't. That was it for her talent, though. She'd been encouraged to write and tried: sitting in front of a blank page and squeezing her head as if juicing it. She couldn't sing, or draw, or act, but she could react like all getout.

It amused her, with Rafael, to be told once again that she was sharp for her age. He was twenty-seven. He'd returned his cousin's car, a bit late the next day, and then soon—way too soon, maybe—was spending most of his free time in her apartment. Norah couldn't think of a good reason to forbid it: he was tidy, considerate, charming in bed and out.

"I should warn you that I might go home to Duluth."

"Doolooze," Rafa said, making it sound like a place in France. "I'd go there. I'd follow you anywhere, Norah."

She winced; he was too young to realize how false such words sounded, even if he thought he meant them. He didn't read newspapers, which shocked her; though her aversion to cell phones made him laugh. They walked holding hands through the plaza, stopping to kiss like teenagers.

American tourists came daily to admire its village-like charm but didn't seem to realize that they were in it—they wore soft, pajama-ish outfits as if they were at home, looking at Spain on TV. Not that she and Rafa were inconspicuous, making out in the street.

"Spanish men," Norah heard a woman say, in English. "I'm like to faint."

"Blonde girl's a looker," a man with her said.

"She's no girl."

Norah didn't think Rafa had heard this until he said later, "I thought looker means prostitute."

"It's a compliment from when I was a girl on the prairie, sonny," she said, in a Midwestern old-lady voice. She'd decided it was best to make a joke of the fifteen years between them.

Before Rafa, she'd never known a Spanish man who was always in a good mood, who didn't sulk or bully waiters and taxi drivers, who didn't put a hand on her thigh and then turn to flirt with the woman next to him. His habit of waking up with a smile on his face baffled her, until she remembered that she'd been accused, in the past, of unnatural cheeriness. My little prairie milkmaid, the Socialist had said, touching her cheek. And then, with the same caress, my little prairie cow.

Norah didn't tell him that story; she told him a funny one about when she first went grocery shopping in Spain. She'd asked if a jar of jam had *preservativos* in it, learning later that *preservativos* are condoms.

"Speaking of which," she said, "we could get a blood test and throw those nasty things away."

"You'd like to have a baby?"

He said it as if proposing ice cream cones. "I can't," Norah said. This was what a doctor in San Sebastian had told her, long ago. The novelist had taken it into his head to have a child with her, and insisted she see a specialist when no baby materialized.

"What about adopting one? I'd help you take care of it," Rafa said eagerly, a boy making wild promises about a puppy. Norah bit her cheek not to laugh and hurt his feelings. It seemed that during his whole childhood in Seville, nobody ever had—he had the sunniest memories.

"*Mi infancia son recuerdos de un patio de Sevilla*," Norah quoted. It was her favorite Spanish poem.

"My mother's, too!" Rafa exclaimed. "She'll love you," he said. Norah had enough experience with Spanish mothers to know this would not be true, but she was surprised when a package of homemade sweets arrived—he'd given his mother this address! –with a note in a fine, spidery script instructing Rafa, somewhat ambiguously, to share.

He had dozens of ex-girlfriends, who flew in and out of the apartment like bright canaries. They adored him; they adored Norah, too. She was the one for him; they'd never seen him like this! Norah was happy to hand out beers and humor them all.

"When do I get to meet your friends?" Rafa said. He looked at her sidelong. "Are you keeping them secret, or me?"

"Rafael Balboa—I've just bought his CD," Eva said. She and Norah were drinking coffee at the Cervecería Alemana, a favorite of Hemingway's salad days, and of theirs, too. The mounted bulls' heads on the walls were bald in patches, like beloved stuffed toys.

"You predicted it," Norah said, and Eva looked blank. "Remember? You saw a musician in the cards, that day in the Reina Victoria."

"Did I? An easy guess," Eva said. "Since every other man in Spain is a musician. I suppose he's a nightmare to live with, though—dishes full of fag ends and demanding perfectly rumpled shirts for his performances?"

"He smokes on the balcony," Norah said. "He knows five pasta recipes by heart."

"When does he return to his planet?" Eva said, though she'd once been quite serious about extraterrestrial life.

"I thought you'd tell me. A love triangle was the other part of your prediction."

Eva's expression became distant. "It's interesting that the triangle symbolizes both stability and change," she said.

"Well, obviously," Norah said, impatient with the misty tone Eva took on when she acted professional. "Why don't you and Juan come to dinner Friday, before the spaceship takes Rafa back?" She thought this would be preferable to a meal at Juan's place—slipping up and mysteriously knowing her way to the bathroom.

"Lovely. You don't mind cooking without salt or cream, do you? He's developed a very boring heart condition."

"Oh, Eva, I'm so sorry!" Norah cried. How often, over the last ten years, had she longed to say those words! She'd fretted, justified herself, and apologized; around and around like a rosary. Occasionally, walking on a Barcelona street, she'd discovered that her lips were moving.

"Juan's not dead, Norah, just older."

* * *

"That's a nice dress," Rafa said, from the bed, as Norah tried on a long, slinky purple skirt. He gave her a sly smile. "Do you fancy this Juan?"

"He's old," Norah said, then realized she'd skated onto dangerous ice.

"He's a famous Spanish womanizer for the past hundred years, I think."

"Not any more," Norah said earnestly. "Eva's all he wants. He told me so, once, after they'd quarreled."

This wasn't a lie, though she'd left out the part about falling into bed with Juan and their both realizing, about an hour later, that it was a mistake.

"It was a good deed for you to get them back together," Rafa said. He leaned back against the pillows with his guitar.

Eva arrived, alone, dressed in an odd black dress with drapey fringe, like a witch costume. "Juan never told me until ten minutes ago that he had to go on that chat show tonight," she said.

He's avoiding me deliberately, Norah thought. So was she going to be haunted, endlessly, for that one mistake? Wouldn't it be better to come out with the truth? No: that's pure selfishness. It was her grandmother's voice she heard, taut as the lid of a Mason jar.

"Norah, you're ravishing," Eva said. "Love becomes you."

Rafa came slouching out of the bedroom, not even changed out of his sweaty T-shirt. He made Norah a liar by not lifting a finger to help with the meal. Instead he sat, pashalike, blowing smoke rings, waiting to be served. Why hadn't she noticed before how he jiggled his feet and fiddled with things at the table, how he wiped his mouth with the back of his wrist and talked over people and interrupted?

And Eva! She seemed mad, prattling—that was the only word for it—about a new thing she was into called soul travel, where you trained your soul to leave your body and fly around the universe, communing with other souls, the souls of the living and the dead. Many people in different parts of the world had experienced this phenomenon. She was going to a conference about it in Budapest.

"Are you going by soul or by plane?" Rafa asked.

Norah went to the kitchen to make coffee. Even the food had been a disaster: the salt-free, fat-free spaghetti she'd made for Juan's sake tasted like rubber bands.

When she came back with the tray, Eva was sitting beside Rafa on the sofa, laying out his cards on the coffee table: he would have career success, an important journey, a new love. "Now, a new love doesn't necessarily mean a new lover," Eva said, glancing at Norah. "It could be a new job, a new hobby—even a new pet."

She saw Eva turn over the seven of hearts, which meant, if Norah remembered correctly, that someone in the room was harboring secret thoughts. Well, here was hers: if Eva was truly clairvoyant, why did she think Rafa was being anything but polite?

He stood up, yawning loudly. "I must get back to my practicing," he said.

"He's not usually like this," Norah said, as the bedroom door closed.

"He's young," Eva said, shrugging. "Shall we catch the last bit of Juan?"

They turned on the TV just as Juan was coming to the end of a remark about America that made the audience burst into wild applause. The camera moved in on his face, and his dark-blue eyes glittered in a way that reminded Norah that eyes are set in skulls. "He looks well," she said, to hide her shock that he didn't.

"Yes; I think the new tablets are helping," Eva said.

After she left, Norah said, "I'm afraid you didn't see the real Eva."

"She's nice," Rafa said. He was stacking plates and carrying them to the kitchen, whistling, as if his soul had traveled from his body for the evening, promising to be back in time for the washing up.

Norah thought Eva's predictions for Rafa were probably right on all counts, but that his new love would not be a dog or a cat. No: it would be a woman who could stay awake past ten o'clock. Suddenly, Norah couldn't—she'd doze off anywhere, even in clubs with the smoke thick and the music blaring. Love had exhausted her, finally. Wouldn't it be better if she conceded now, rather than after her fresh, young replacement appeared? "I'm too old for you," she said.

Rafa just laughed at her. "You're not old."

"For you I am." She kept at it; digging her own grave, patiently, with a teaspoon.

"All right! You're old. You're way, way, way too old! You're a raisin."

"See?"

She went to bed whenever she could. After lunch, she even put on her pajamas. You could do this in Spain; the siesta was still part of life here, much as government and trade officials denied it. Norah's dreams were ones where she stood rooted, unable to dodge disaster. She'd wake as if drugged, eat a whole bag of potato chips or a half-pint of ice cream and then crawl back under the covers. At least Rafa wouldn't betray her in her own bed, because she was always in it.

One afternoon, she woke to hear the five o'clock bells chiming in the plaza. She'd slept through her afternoon class. She threw on her clothes and ran across the square toward the bus stop, raising clouds of indignant pigeons. But then she had to stop and put her hand on the back of a bench; she was dizzy with hunger. She went into a *confitería* and bought a cream-filled *brazo de niño*—the most delicious pastry in Spain, in spite of the gruesome name: arm of child. She stood on the sidewalk devouring it, though eating on the street is considered disgusting; only beggars and Americans do it.

She was licking her fingers when she saw Eva walking toward her, looking like a gypsy princess with her hair and skirt and silk scarves fluttering behind her in the breeze. "How are you, Norah?"

"Strange. I feel strange." Her words took her by surprise. She touched her cheeks, which were puffy with sleep and salty snacks.

Eva put her hand on Norah's arm. "Did you think you could be pregnant?"

"I couldn't be." Yet what else explained her constant, heavy sleepiness, her almost crazed hunger, her sensation of moving slowly through a liquefied world?

"Well—" Eva began, laughing a little. "I take it Rafa doesn't know."

"It never occurred to me, until you said so." Her momentary, ravenous elation faded. She felt sick.

"He'll be very happy," Eva said.

"Sudden fertility at advanced maternal age is a well-known phenomenon," the doctor in the walk-in clinic told Norah. "Or perhaps the problems you were told you had never existed. San Sebastian doctors," he snorted, as if they were well-known quacks. "But still, a miracle at age forty-two."

"Not in a biblical sense," Norah said. "I have been having sex." Had, was more like it. All she did now was eat and sleep, as if she were a baby herself.

"Do you know who the father is?"

She nodded; too tired to be outraged.

* * *

Norah called Rafa's cell phone; a thing she rarely did. But she dreaded seeing even a flicker of dismay at her news. "A baby—fantastic!" he cried, over the din of the street.

"I'm relieved you think so."

"How could I not be happy about a baby? And you know, I have good news, too. I got the contract to make the CD in Seville, after all."

"After all?"

"Didn't I tell you? Just as your friend predicted. It will be a live recording—all in the bars and cafes of the old city. A truly authentic sound. We'll finish in a month or two, if everything goes well. I'm leaving tomorrow."

"Of course you are," Norah said, and hung up.

It was after midnight when she woke to Rafa's key in the lock; the thump of his guitar case on the floor. She'd cried for hours, until she was distilled down to a single, mammalian notion: it was the child she'd wanted, all along.

He entered the dark bedroom, the air of which, Norah supposed, was still humid with emotion. "I don't have to go to Seville," he said at once. "I'll cancel."

"I'd like you to go," Norah said. "I'd rather be alone just now."

"*Bueno*," was all he said, and then they both lay silent and awake for hours, like two rolled-up carpets. He'd fallen asleep when she rose at dawn. She washed her face in cold water and went out with her book bag into the cool, pink morning.

Oh, Madrid! If she couldn't successfully love any man, she could at least love this place, to the point where she was unable to distinguish its flaws from its virtues: its mingled odors of diesel smoke, fried garlic, jasmine, and fish heads; the tall, splashing fountains built with conquistador plunder, the tiny cars packed like mosaic tiles around every traffic circle. She loved teaching English, too: its brick-solid novels, its wayward, illogical grammar. All day she loved everything, giddy with insomnia and caffeine.

She walked home in the gold evening light, and when she crossed the Plaza Santa Ana she saw Rafa standing with his backpack beside the taxi stand of the Reina Victoria, smoking. She started to hurry toward him. She'd wish him goodbye; good luck—she felt that if she just stood near him he would be swept by the happiness washing over her; it was that strong, like magnetism or a tide. But he didn't seem to see her. He threw away his cigarette and went into the hotel.

She went out on her balcony and watched the entrance until Rafa came out again. He got into a taxi, which rounded the corner and headed south, toward the train station. Norah called Eva's suite.

"How lovely to hear you, Norah! But I've got a client, actually."

"It's your last visitor I'm calling about," Norah said. "Did you forget, Eva, that my balcony is right across the plaza?"

"I told Rafa he oughtn't to come on the sly," Eva said, sounding quite cool.

"What other way would he? With my blessing?"

"He knows you don't think much of what I do. Same as I know it. You're not good at hiding your opinions, Norah."

"You read his cards?"

"I've known you too long to feel insulted. Mostly, I feel sorry for you."

"You should," Norah said. "Because I'm completely pathetic." She burst into tears. "Please forgive me, Eva."

"Of course," Eva said. "Look, I've got to go, but one day you might want to see the cards that foretell you and me sitting out on those benches. Two foreign old ladies taking the air."

The next morning, Norah felt calm, sitting with her mug of tea on the balcony as the sun gilded the facades of the buildings opposite. There was, she noticed for the first time, a swing set on the plaza.

A week passed; then two. Norah had tea with Eva, who laid out cards for her baby but didn't mention its errant father. After a month had gone by, Norah concluded that she wouldn't see or hear from Rafa again. She taught her English classes; she cooked nutritious, leafy meals; she took walks on the raked footpaths in Retiro Park, where she smiled at the well-dressed, perfumed Spanish children. A letter arrived from her mother (her parents had never gotten the hang of e-mail) with details of their winter visit. They were looking forward to meeting her musical friend.

Norah guessed they'd receive her decision, her baby, with enthusiasm and affection—she could do no wrong, in their doting eyes. She wished, not for the first time, that it were possible to truly be the person they saw. She folded her letter and turned her face to the sun. Then she felt herself drifting, lying on a dock. A screen door banged; ice clinked in glasses; she heard the excited squeak of a child pulling up minnows in a net. She was on the shore of Lake Superior in summer, in her future. Spain was the past, but even considering this idea in a dream was unbearable.

Minnesota blackflies buzzed near her ear; she batted at them until she realized the sound she heard was her apartment intercom, in Madrid.

"I've lost my key!" It was Rafa, calling up from the street. Norah stood up and peered over the balcony. Beside him was a gray-haired woman in widow's black whose iron profile showed what his would be when he lost all his optimism. But now he was grinning up at her, as if he'd just awakened from another of his enjoyable dreams and spotted her, exactly where he'd left her the night before.

If you think you can just come waltzing back, without a by-your-leave.

Obviously, Rafa and his mother intended to stand on the sidewalk until Norah, or some unsuspecting neighbor, let them in. She pressed the buzzer. From the landing she watched the old woman climb the stairs ahead of her son. Actually, she wasn't all that elderly, Norah realized—maybe closer to her in age than Rafa was. She had the purposeful bearing of someone who expected, and possibly relished, disappointment. We've got that in common, *Señora*. This thought made her smile.

Later that day, Rafa said he'd never forget how Norah looked leaning over the stair railing—beaming at him like Rapunzel, with her gold hair hanging down.

hands. And here's Osama bin Laden, another kid from her year. He'd have been the rich stoner: aloof, mocking. Crazy parties at his place—his parents were always out of town.

The rest of the magazine articles are about ordinary people cursed, like Bible characters: they've been savaged by their employers, their neighbors' dogs, or their own malevolent genes. But they soldier on, thanks to courage Priscilla knows she'd never be able to muster. They have orange plaid sofas, terrible haircuts—not their fault, prairie dwellers surrounded by factory outlets, but wouldn't people change out of their sweats, at least, if photographers were coming?

She's studied every printed word in the room now; even the arthritis drug brochures and the warnings on the biohazard bins, and still no doctor. In the hallway outside, like the rumble of trucks, are men's voices. She'd asked for a women's practice, but the HMO must have run out of them. Twenty—ten—years ago, she'd have marched out to the front desk to complain, paper robe or no, but she no longer believes her body is her self. It's just a vehicle; her private car. And male doctors must be different now, too: not like old Dr. Macnab, who, when she asked for birth control pills at seventeen said he was afraid he'd have to tell her folks. Never mind then, she'd said. He's dead now, and the boy who waited for her at the bicycle rack outside the clinic lives in Africa; he and his wife run an AIDS prevention program. But neither of them knew much about prevention that day; though they should've, both in Advanced Placement biology—they seemed to think they'd come out of the doctor's office with the goods like it was a nickel bag; that they'd go up into the foothills on their bikes and eat a pill and everything would be groovy. They'd ditched school for what they'd thought was going to be this event, but they were both too intent on college to take chances, so they went to a matinee of *Hearts and Minds* instead, and the lust just drained right out of them.

Finally, a hand on the doorknob. Rumble, rumble, says the doc, to a passing nurse. She stops with a jingle, like a reindeer braking. Rumble. Rumble. Meanwhile, Priscilla's thighs are taking on a bluish, turkeyleg look. She's been assigned to a Dr. Green. Well, at least he's thorough; nattering on and on to the nurse like that. Not that she expects him to find anything wrong with her. She's here simply because she hasn't had a physical in ages; she's in that medical stretch of time, hopefully decades long, between when she's stopped having babies and her final, fatal illness. Making the appointment had nagged at her like a thank-you note so overdue that actually writing it becomes impossible. Then suddenly, a trapdoor in her life opened, though this surely isn't what her friends meant by getting out more. Massage has been recommended, but she's in no mood to be caressed by strangers. And there again, the problem of how much to undress.

Ah, Dr. Green! He sails in, white coat flapping. Jolly, portly—Louisa May Alcott words—come to mind. Bald, but for a carpet-strip of curls, the color of hamster bedding, above the ears. He extends his hand to her, and his fingers are warm, thank heavens.

"Mrs. Mott?"

"Ms." But she grins, to show she's not a humorless feminist; bra-burners, they used to be called. She'd see them yelling on the TV news.

"Castrating," Priscilla's father had said.

"What?" She was ten.

"Robert," her mother said mildly. "Like what the vet did to Sparky, sweetheart, so he wouldn't run away."

The doctor looks at her chart, then at her. "Priscilla?"

Another wry smile. In classrooms filled with Tracis and Stacis and Kimmis, there she was, with a name like a Pilgrim hat. Her older brother drew Cilli, in psychedelic letters, with the dot of the 'I' made into a flaming sun, on her binder, and she thanked him and almost went to school with it until she said it aloud to herself a few times. Now she likes her name; it's rare, for somebody her age.

This is apparently what Dr. Green thinks, as he rechecks her chart and then her mid-forties face. "You look the same as ever, Pris," he says finally.

Then she recognizes him, too.

"Charlie?" There's some resemblance, about as strong as a Halloween mask of a President. But those are definitely Charlie's blue eyes, peering out at her. She strips away a hundred pounds; adds a mop of luxuriant blond hair, a faded Sticky Fingers t-shirt, and he comes into focus, as if the optometrist has found the right lens. "Goodness, so do you! But Dr. Green? Did you take your wife's last name, then?"

He looks at the ring on his plump finger and smiles tenderly, as if that were his wife, thin and golden. Remarried, she thinks. "Green was my mother's maiden name," he says. "I changed it when I realized being Dr. Dykman was a bit of a non-starter with the female patients."

"Oh, sure. Funny how I never even thought about your last name, in college."

"In grade school, high school, I was teased mercilessly. Then later, in med school. But in college, for some reason, people didn't."

"Everyone was too busy having sex to make jokes about it." Charlie—Dr. Green—just looks at her, and she's conscious of having no underwear on, and sitting with her knees almost touching the belly of this fat man who used to be a skinny boy she'd had sex with. Rather a lot of sex, spring quarter of senior year. She was pretty sure of Phi Beta Kappa, but not at all of her future. The end of the sexual revolution was at hand, though nobody knew it—or maybe they did, in the way squirrels know a hard winter's coming.

"Still the same Priscilla, with her comments," the doctor says.

"Comments?"

"The things you came out with. Some people admired that. You didn't seem to care what anyone thought of you."

"Why, what did people think of me?"

Charlie appears to be considering how to answer; his expression becomes the one he probably assumes when the lab results aren't quite what were hoped for. "Just kidding," she says. "I don't really want to know."

"And what are we seeing you for today?" He scans the chart she filled out at Reception.

"Gee." She didn't know she had to have a specific complaint. She'd imagined that a physical would be like a facial; that she'd walk in and they'd bend over her, murmuring soothingly in Hungarian, and set to work. "My 588-month check-up, I guess."

"Ah-ha. Still quite the wit, are you, Pris."

Quite the wit? Was that how Charlie talked, back then? She can't recall. Drugs, her husband would say, shaking his head. She didn't do drugs; well, not many, and neither did he, but it amuses him to pretend they did. "Purple Haze," he'll say, when asked what they've been doing, at a cocktail party. He comes out with things; they have that in common. For instance, he'd come out with the fact that his old girl-friend drove down from Baltimore to look for a suit to wear for her second wedding, over the long weekend she'd taken the kids to California to see their grandma.

"She came to Washington to shop for clothes?" Priscilla had said, incredulous about the wrong thing entirely. Having lived in New York in her twenties has made her a theoretical snob about stores, though most of her stuff is from Target.

Her husband had come out with the fact that the old girl-friend didn't find anything she liked, actually, but that they'd had a good lunch at the Vietnamese place. Then Priscilla found that pearl earring, burrowed like a tick in the fur of the sheepskin mat on her side of the bed. She set it on his pillow: a hotel chocolate.

"Oh, wow," he said, in his mock-druggy voice, then burst into tears.

"I haven't been sleeping well," she tells Charlie. "Maybe I need some pills?" But it's unlikely that pills would help. It's not that she's tossing and turning; it's that she's up all night, yelling. Yelling in whispers, with kids in the next room. Then she collapses, spent, at first light, to sleep an hour or two before she has to hustle everyone to the school bus stop.

"You can have an affair," her husband had said, desperate at two a.m. His bedrock sense of fairness was one of the virtues she'd praised, long ago, in their premarital session with the minister.

"I don't want one." Priscilla conjured up a lurid perp walk of the other men in her life: dishwasher repairmen, middle school principals. Probably, she's not their cup of tea, either. But she was Charlie's, once, and here she is, breathing heavily as her former lover listens to her lungs, her heart, his head so close she could reach out and crush it to her partially-exposed breasts.

"You might be a bit run down, but I don't think drugs are the answer," Charlie says.

"Charlie Dykman doesn't think drugs are the answer? That's a riot."

He gazes at her reproachfully. "People change, Priscilla."

"You seem to believe that you've changed, while I haven't."

He smiles. "Touché. Fact is, you haven't, much. For a premenopausal woman—"

"Why is everybody pre-something, all of a sudden? Can't you just be what you are right this minute? My daughter's ten, and she keeps being told she's a pre-teenager. Are we going to start calling people with cancer pre-dead?"

Charlie gives her a look you might give someone wheeling all her earthly possessions down the street in a shopping cart. He reaches again for the chart. "That reminds me, you forgot to answer this question here. Is there a family history of cancer?"

"It's not history," Priscilla says. "It's a current event."

She and Charlie discuss her mother's case. Like many people her age, she's become—suddenly, unwillingly—an amateur oncologist. "I'd say her prospects sound good," Charlie says.

"Good's not good enough. I've always aimed for outstanding."

"Which is how I'd describe your overall health picture. Married, kids, part-time work, that's excellent, medically speaking. Are you still with—Steve, was it?"

"Yup." She's surprised Charlie knows whom she married, since she'd lost track of him completely. "Still with Steve." She says this almost apologetically, the way parents of only children do. Maybe that's why she hasn't thrown Steve out; believed him when he said this is the one time he's transgressed; been moved by all those tears—he's a spoiled-rotten only husband. And maybe that's why she can't forgive him, either: she doesn't have anyone else to distract her attention.

"A happy marriage is huge, healthwise," Charlie says. "I envy the way you've aged, frankly, Pris, and if I'm honest with myself I'll admit that's why I probably insist on thinking of you as a tactless, lascivious twenty-one-year-old."

"Lascivious?" She clutches her paper dress closed at the neck.

"You hid it well, under a prim demeanor. Still do, I see. Perhaps you'd prefer to have a nurse-practitioner do the gynecological exam."

"I should say so!"

The nurse, a lowly vassal in this office kingdom, doesn't make her wait. She comes in, keys and thermometers clinking gaily, just as Charlie's leaving. She's tiny, with big dark eyes under a heavy fringe of black hair. He halts, as if she were blocking his way with stern bulk, and turns back.

"Priscilla," he says, suddenly tentative, as if he were standing in the doorway of her room for the first time, with two mugs of Red Zinger tea. "I'd like you to meet my wife, Jessie Green. Jessie, this is Priscilla Mott. She was one of the members of the group house I told you about, in college."

"Amazing," Jessie says. Priscilla shakes her hand, a mouse's paw. She looks thirteen; wears a gold cross at her throat— clearly, not as a fashion accessory.

"Great to see you, Pris. Whatever you're doing, keep it up. It obviously agrees with you."

"Great to see you, too," she says. "Dr. Dykman," she mutters, as the door closes behind him. Priscilla doesn't know what's annoyed her most: tactless, lascivious, or this baby wife.

"This may be a bit uncomfortable," Jessie says.

"Oh, please. I had three children without anesthesia."

"Whoa." The big eyes get bigger. "Why?"

She shrugs. "I don't trust doctors."

She lies back, and after a few seconds Jessie says softly, "So you're one of the folks who knew Charlie back in his wild days?"

She squeaks. "Sorry," Jessie says.

Priscilla sits up. "It was before you were born, probably."

"I'm twenty-seven," Jessie says stiffly.

"Oh, like—"she waves her hand dismissively at the pile of magazines on the counter—Katie Holmes."

"Charlie's always said I look like Liv Tyler," Jessie says.

Priscilla tilts her head and nods. "Sure! I see it."

"You look like an actress, too. I can't think of her name. She's British."

"Oh, right. The older lady with the bad teeth?"

"No, she—" Jessie flushes. "I'll bet you were cute in college," she says, a little despairingly. "Are you the one who wrote poems?"

"Yeah, but I've been clean for years now." A flicker of hurt passes over Jessie's face, and then Priscilla sees her rise above it, right before her eyes.

"Look, Jessie," she says. "You're young, but you're old enough to understand it doesn't matter, what people did in college. It has no bearing."

"My college experience has bearing. That's when I welcomed Jesus Christ into my life."

"Ah." Priscilla tries hard for a neutral, nonjudgemental sound. "What does Charlie think of your religion?"

"Think? I met him at church."

This is astounding, but also the only plausible explanation for the gulf between what Charlie is and what he was. Priscilla wants the old, golden-haired Charlie back, but she realizes that Charlie would've had no idea what to say to a middle-aged woman like her, worried sick about her even older mother. "I can't believe he's a Christian," she says.

"Aren't you?"

"Well, yes, but not by choice. I wonder how it makes his mother feel." She remembers Mrs. Dykman: a small, opinionated woman, who'd escaped from Vienna as a child.

"She'd just died of leukemia when Charlie started attending. Plus his marriage was breaking up, the whole nine yards. Some people, the Lord really has to smite to get their attention."

"Oh." Priscilla hates talk like this, of a punishing God, banging his fist on the dinner table. That's why she doesn't believe. But she feels bad, wanting greedily for her mother to be in perfect health—she's alive, and Charlie's isn't. And Priscilla didn't even ask about her. Oh, she's greedy, vain, selfish, lascivious—she's got every deadly sin. But she's going to have to live with them, without anesthesia, because, though she's often wished she could, over the years, she can't believe.

She looks around for her clothes, like a call girl who's never in the same room twice. "Please tell Charlie how sorry

I am about his mother. She made delicious poppy seed cookies, I remember."

"Charlie makes them now," Jessie says. "We'll send you a card, Mrs. Mott, if we find anything abnormal. If you don't hear from us, assume you're fine."

"Then I hope I never hear from you again." Like much of what Priscilla says, these days, this sounds worse than what she meant, but Jessie gives her one quick, brilliant, forgiving smile. So Charlie has that, she thinks.

Then she drives home, instead of to work, figuring she can make the hours up next week, if nobody catches the strep that's going around school, that is, and makes pot roast with cream of mushroom soup instead of the tofu thing she was planning, and brownies with shredded coconut—magic brownies, Steve likes to call them, though of course the kids don't know why—and she listens to her favorite music all afternoon, which is her children's favorite, too, because they're still too young to rebel against her ancient, pointless rebellion; they think, when Mick Jagger sings about Mother's Little Helper, that it's about them setting the table.

tinean workmen couldn't understand what Walter was saying, however, and while he was busy searching through the packing boxes for his typewriter, I had them carry the table through to the dining room.

I didn't want to move. I already loved the flat, despite having discovered its flaws—the odor of mildew no amount of lye could remove from the kitchen tiles, the bath pipes that groaned and trembled when the taps were opened. But the rooms, though not large, were full of the soft light of the far south. In the parlor and dining room there were French windows which still held their original panes of beveled glass, and their brass handles were in the shape of dolphins plunging into surf. There had been window pulls exactly like them in my father's house in Frankfurt. Turning those dolphins in my hands comforted me, and when the windows were opened I could lean out onto a patio filled with jacaranda trees. It was October when we moved into the flat; springtime in Argentina—every morning the parquet was littered with violet blossoms. I wouldn't let the maid sweep them up.

But for my husband, who was a philosopher by profession, fish-shaped doorknobs and purple flowers on the floor were not good reasons to share a staircase with people who might have waved flags as Hitler passed on parade. I argued that with our son, Gabriel, turning fifteen and entering the Liceo across the street, abandoning the flat would have amounted to a victory for *them*. I pointed to the floor as I spoke. (We never referred to our downstairs neighbors as the Schmidts, or the Germans. They were nameless pronouns, always.)

Walter nodded slowly. "Just promise me, Greta, that you'll never, ever greet him, nor his wife." And so I promised. That afternoon, he typed out a letter to an organization in New York that hunted war criminals.

Yes, they knew about our neighbor. But he'd had a trivial desk job; they had bigger fish to fry. He looked mild enough, shuffling down the passage with his library book and a furled umbrella, but that's what everybody said about Eichmann, wasn't it? It was the sight of her that distressed me in a way I couldn't explain.

I imagined she'd been pretty as a girl. She had the features that had been so praised in our country—the planed cheekbones, the round blue eyes, the butter-colored hair— but they'd flattened and faded so that she resembled an overworked farm animal. Frivolously, perhaps, I felt there was justice in the fact that as the years passed I remained slender; that I kept a smooth olive skin, and my hair, as it grayed, stayed thick and curly.

In thirty years, I never saw her with a female friend. No callers. Nobody ringing their bell at teatime, or even at their Christmas. Once, I admitted feeling sorry for her. "There are six million who deserve your pity more," Walter exclaimed, throwing down the newspaper.

It was Amanda who informed me that Señora Schmidt used to wait on the upstairs landing until after I'd gone out to market in the morning, before setting out herself. "It's like she's afraid of you, Señora," the concierge said, keeping her eyes on her knitting. "There's people who still don't like the

Jews, but I always tell about you and Señor Walter as an example of why they're wrong."

"Well, thank you," I replied, wondering if she were leaning over the banister and listening.

I'd walk down the narrow cobbled lanes of the San Telmo district to the marketplace, knowing she was following a few blocks behind. Two European women at the farthest corner of South America—we lived closer to colonies of penguins than to any other civilized place—did her heart twist at the sight of the stone mermaids on the columns of the house on the corner of Emerald Street, the Gothic spires of the church steeple, the cackling gargoyles under the eaves of the National Bank and the gaily-colored Mercedes-Benz buses?

I was seventeen when Walter took me away with him to Buenos Aires. My father, who refused to see the logic of leaving his very own country, was so angry he barely said goodbye. Now he was dead, as was everyone I'd loved as a girl in Frankfurt. This fact would come to me anew on my walks to the market, like a fresh blast of cold wind off the pampas. There were days when I'd arrive at the market entrance almost blind with grief, before recalling my husband and son, and the provisions I'd set out to buy.

Maybe a brisket of beef to be simmered in wine, with a watercress soup to start? Walnuts to be put into an iced cake for tea. Everything grew beautifully in the rich, dark Argentine soil, and it soothed me to arrange my baskets to look just so, with spinach draped over the sides like green velvet, the grapes and lemons nestled together, a bundle of lilies of the Nile tied to the handle.

Occasionally I'd spot her out of the corner of my eye as she entered the marketplace, her coin purse clutched to her breast as though she expected to be accosted. Her purchases were meager – perhaps a single flayed chop, or a soup bone and a quarter-kilo packet of barley. I'd look away before she noticed me watching her, and set out for home with my over-flowing baskets. Unlike them, we always expected visitors: Walter's students, his editors, and, in later years, his admirers on a pilgrimage from abroad. They filled our flat every after-noon with their cigarette smoke and chatter.

That day I passed her on the stairs, we were white-haired ladies, and still I turned my head. But I'd noticed she was car-rying a plastic bag from the *Farmacia de Milagros*. Walter called it the Miracle Pharmacy. After fifty years in Argentina, he still enjoyed the silliness of Spanish translated literally. We'd had a series of cleaning women—Angustias, Dolores, Remedios—whom he referred to as Anguish, Pains and Remedies. But now that Walter's cancer was so advanced, we'd stopped ex-pecting miracles from the pharmacy; only shelter, *amparo*, which is also a woman's name in Spanish.

Her shopping bag was filled with empty glass vials; I could hear them clacking together as she descended the stairs. She walked out the front door, and I leaned over the railing to watch her hail a taxi. She looked up and down the sidewalk before she got into the cab, clutching her sack with both hands. I sighed and climbed up to our flat with my basket.

Walter was awake. His breathing was noisy, but even. The maid he called Pillar closed her *Hola* magazine and went to the kitchen to make my tea.

"He's in a bad way," I said. I took off my coat, scarf and hat and held them on my lap, as if I were a visitor who didn't plan to stay long. "I saw her taking vials out again today—maybe three dozen."

Walter closed his eyes and opened them. He reminded me, suddenly, of a doll I'd had, long ago. "Argentina is shit," he said.

I thought he meant because of the doctor's warning when he wrote out Walter's prescription for morphine—not to throw the vials out with the household trash. An addict finding them might find us and rob us. "Take a taxi and dispose of them in another part of the city," the doctor had told me. "Make sure nobody follows you when you get into the cab." Luckily, the Americans upstairs took care of that for me, when they went out on their newspaper reporting. They're lovely boys, all three of them. They'd read to Walter when my voice gave out.

"Crime is all over the world, Walter. Imagine if the Americans had given us visas when we asked for them. We might be living in New York now, with all their drug addicts."

"No," Walter said firmly. "This country is shit."

"Don't say that," I begged. "They've given us so much." I recited the blessings he'd listed for me so often, when I was overcome with homesickness and sorrow: our Gabriel, born in Buenos Aires, Walter's university post, his newspaper columns, all our friends, a flat we owned with French windows opening onto jacaranda trees.

"Idiots let it rain on the just and the unjust," Walter said. "How is it that he deserves morphine also?"

I didn't know what to answer. "A man of conscience" is how Walter was described in his obituaries, and he was so not only in his writing. He was attentive to his son; he never failed to greet me tenderly each morning; he'd drop his work to make some small household repair I asked for, after the concierge grew too fat to climb the stairs. He wasn't vain; packets of his clippings would arrive in the mail in languages we didn't even speak, but I was the one who pasted them all into a book.

"Well," I said finally. "The least you can do is outlive him. The Italian lady at the store sent her own soup for you." I held up the mayonnaise jar wrapped in waxed paper.

"All right," Walter said, smiling with his eyes closed.

Though this is not generally admitted, anyone who's sat shiva will agree that it can be a festive time. The bell rang day and night; feet clattered on the stairs; there was nowhere to put all the food. Gabriel and his wife, Sonia, came every day; the journalists played checkers with the grandchildren. Old Amanda hauled herself and half her extended family up the steps; they poured glasses of red wine for everyone and admired the fabric I'd put over the mirrors as if it were some sort of holiday décor.

Finally, though, the last person left and the day came when everything had been eaten. I'd sent Pilar home to her province as a reward for all the dishwashing, and so had to confront the matter of cooking a meal for one person. I put on my coat and hat and got my basket and started down the stairs.

The door to the flat below opened as I reached the landing. Our neighbor had died sometime in the week of Walter's funeral. I don't know if it was the religion or if it was just them, but whatever was observed, had been observed in silence.

Her head popped out—that sad, bovine face. "*Guten tag, Frau Greta,*" she said.

"*Guten tag, Frau Elsa.*"

My cheeks went hot; my heart was beating crazily. I had to steady myself on the railing as I continued down the steps. I went outside, inhaling the diesel fumes in great gasps. But once in the marketplace, I became calm and looked around carefully—at the cabbages, the clean pyramids of potatoes, the hanging red meats. I began to remember recipes; to combine ingredients in my mind; to think of dishes a guest from home might enjoy.

ACKNOWLEDGEMENTS

I WOULD LIKE TO ACKNOWLEDGE THE PUBLICATIONS in which these stories first appeared, some in slightly different form: "You Don't Know Anything," *Flyway* and *Flash Fiction Forward* (Norton); "Aliens" *Timber Creek Review* and *Amazing Graces* (Paycock Press); "Do Not Call," *Baltimore Review*—First Place, Short Fiction Competition; "Flames," *Narrative*; "Milagros," *Narrative Magazine*; "Teardown," *Bethesda Magazine*; "Miguel Rivera," *New South*; "Looker," *River Oak Review*; "Class Notes," *Baltimore Review*; "The Nazi Wife," *Byline*.

I am indebted to fellow writers James Mathews, Carmelinda Blagg, Catherine Bell, Jim Beane, Dana Cann, Madelyn Rosenberg, Christina Kovac, Susan Land and Paula Delgado-Kling who responded to repeated incarnations of these stories with patience, wisdom and good humor. Thanks also to Tom Jenks and Olga Zilberbourg of *Narrative* for their support and encouragement; to Rich Peabody, a one-man marching band for D.C. area writing. I am lucky to live in a state that vigorously supports the arts and thank the Maryland State Arts Council for three individual artist grants.

Thanks also to Elisavietta Ritchie for urging me to persevere and work even harder on this collection, and to the multi-talented and welcoming folks at WWPH: Elizabeth Bruce, Patric Pepper, David Ebenbach, David Taylor, Melanie Hatter, Brandel France de Bravo.

Finally, gratitude and love to my parents, who took me traveling before I could walk, and to David, Ben, and Alex, who made every place we went feel like home.

CPSIA information can be obtained at www.ICGtesting.com
Printed in the USA
BVOW07s0228241013

334502BV00001B/28/P

P. M. Roget